A Letter to My Son

A Letter to My Son
Kim S.

Trafford Publishing

Order this book online at www.trafford.com/03-2238
or email orders@trafford.com

Most Trafford titles are also available at major online book retailers.

Copy editing: Jennifer Nault, Calgary, AB
Front and back cover photography: Juan Houston, Visions Illustrated, Calgary, AB
Cosmetics: Jackie Johnson Makeup Artistry, Calgary, BC
Graphic design: Trafford Publishing, Victoria, BC
Special thanks to M. Foley and www.brokenspirits.com

25% of author royalties from this book will be donated to the following national mental health
associations: for copies sold in Canada: the CAnadian Mental Health Association (CMHA),
Toronto, ON; for copies sold in the United States: the National Mental Health Association
(NMHA), Alexandria, VA

25% of author royalties from this book will be donated to the following national domestic
violence/abuse associations: for copies sold in Canada: the Canadian Centre from Abuse Awareness
(CCAA), Newmarket, ON; for copies sold in the United States: the National Coalition Against
Domestic Violence (NCADV), Denver, CO.

Note for Librarians: A cataloguing record for this book is available from Library
and Archives Canada at www.collectionscanada.ca/amicus/index-e.html

Printed in Victoria, BC, Canada.

ISBN: 978-1-4120-1860-9

*We at Trafford believe that it is the responsibility of us all, as both individuals
and corporations, to make choices that are environmentally and socially sound.
You, in turn, are supporting this responsible conduct each time you purchase a
Trafford book, or make use of our publishing services. To find out how you are
helping, please visit www.trafford.com/responsiblepublishing.html*

*Our mission is to efficiently provide the world's finest, most comprehensive
book publishing service, enabling every author to experience success.
To find out how to publish your book, your way, and have it available
worldwide, visit us online at www.trafford.com/10510*

 www.trafford.com

North America & international
toll-free: 1 888 232 4444 (USA & Canada)
phone: 250 383 6864 ♦ fax: 250 383 6804 ♦ email: info@trafford.com

The United Kingdom & Europe
phone: +44 (0)1865 722 113 ♦ local rate: 0845 230 9601
facsimile: +44 (0)1865 722 868 ♦ email: info.uk@trafford.com

10 9 8 7

"Good timber does not grow with ease;
the stronger the wind, the stronger the trees."
– J. Willard Marriott

For my mom: the tallest tree in the forest.
Your example keeps me growing.

Contents

"Abby" Remembered

All I remember is the babysitter coming to pick me up from my friend's house. She seemed concerned, and told me that my mother had taken my father to the hospital. I knew dad had been sick for the last two years, but no one really knew what was wrong with him, only that he was exhausted and depressed, unable to continue working. I'd heard some conversations between mom and other adults, something about testing him for diabetes, but I was only eleven years old, so it was difficult to piece everything together. Now, he was in the hospital, and that's all anyone would tell me. I was very confused by it all.

When my mother returned, she was noticeably shaken. I took my seat at the dinner table with my mother and two older brothers, Michael and Alex. We were eating chicken-noodle soup and the room was disturbingly quiet — aside from the occasional sniffle — as we all tried to be brave. "Your father almost died today," mom said. My throat tightened on cue. I got up from the table and ran to the private comfort of the bathroom, unable to face her grief.

It wasn't long before I heard the expected tapping on the door and my mom's sympathetic voice asking me to open it. I let her in and resumed my seat on the toilet, while she knelt down in front of me. To this day, I can see her wet eyes as she spoke, but I don't recall her words. All I knew was that my dad was very sick, had been taken by ambulance to a hospital in Saskatoon, and would be staying there awhile.

Mom took us to visit dad once he was up to it. It seemed like an eternity before we could see him, but it was likely only a matter of days. The hospital in the city was huge compared to the one in our hometown,

Lanigan. I stuck close to mom as we walked down the bright, sterile corridors, afraid of losing her in the maze.

When we reached the visitors' lounge, dad was there waiting for us, smiling and more sociable than he'd been in months. Mom and dad talked while my brothers and I watched some of the other patients on the ward, cracking jokes about one man who couldn't stop shaking and another who sat in a corner on the floor, rocking back and forth. It was all quite amusing because I didn't understand the situation, and I didn't see my father in the same light.

After a while, dad returned home, apparently fully recovered. He was on some sort of medication, in better spirits than he'd been in months, and was finally able to return to work at the local potash mine. Slowly, once he got back on track, he added other activities to his regime. One of them was yard work — we had one of the most beautiful lawns in town — and the other was carpentry.

Dad had always been an early riser, sometimes waking as early as six o'clock in the morning. He'd have his coffee, read the newspaper, and then retire to his workshop in the basement. It was there that he'd built both of my brothers' roll-top desks before he became ill. Now he was going to build mine.

On Saturdays, he usually gave us kids until nine or ten in the morning before starting up his power saw. My bedroom was almost directly above his workshop, so I awoke to that sound every weekend. I'd throw on my robe, then join him downstairs to check on the progress of my desk. We spent a lot of time together down there. I watched him assemble the pieces of oak, sometimes helping him with simple chores, such as sanding and sweeping, so I could feel included in the process.

My relationship with my parents was casual, and I spent a great deal of time talking with them both. Every night before bedtime, it was customary that I join them in their bedroom to give them an overview of my day.

One night in particular, mom wasn't in the room, so I sat at the edge of the bed near my dad. He had a pensive look in his eyes. Dad set his magazine aside, and we had our first honest conversation about his illness.

He initiated the dialogue with, "Do you know why I was in the hospital?"

I shrugged my shoulders. "Because you were sick." That was the extent of my knowledge. He unbuttoned his left cuff link and rolled up his sleeve, pointing to a scar on his inner forearm. It didn't really sink in until later that night, when I was alone in my room and had a chance to think. That someone as gentle as my dad could do something so violent to himself — slice himself like that — made me shudder. I couldn't imagine it. Why hadn't anyone told me before now?

Around the time I started Grade 8, my dad found a job in Saskatoon at the University of Saskatchewan as a boiler room engineer. He moved away before the rest of the family to get settled in his job, staying at his sister Linda's place for a few months. By the time June rolled around and my brothers and I had finished the school year, mom had our house in Lanigan packed up. We were ready to go. It was a time of change for our family, with my eldest brother, Michael, embarking on his first, challenging year of university while I began my first year of high school in the fall. Alex stayed behind to finish Grade 12. Eventually, my mom found work at one of the hospitals in the city and, before long, we were settled in our new home leaving the bleak chapter of dad's illness behind us.

My passage into puberty proved a challenge for mom and dad. As their only daughter and youngest child, I caused them both a few sleepless nights. My father was a bit more tolerant of the teenage bouts of drinking and smoking than my cautious, over-protective mother. As a result, I quickly learned that if I was going to test the limits, it had better be when only he was around.

One time, I got caught smoking in my bedroom when a cigarette I hadn't properly butted out caught fire in my garbage can. Had mom been home at the time, I wouldn't have gotten off as easily as I did. She'd have lectured me on the ill effects of smoking backed by her fifteen years of nursing experience. Instead, my dad chuckled and gave me an ashtray. He told me that if I wanted to smoke, I should keep it down to one or two cigarettes a day.

Dad lived to tease me when I was a teenager. As much as he worried when I was out late, I think it was humorous for him, too. He took such pleasure in taunting my dates when they came to pick me up, staring at them out the living-room window or greeting them at the door just to put them on edge. Then, he'd giggle when I got embarrassed.

One night in particular always comes to mind, always makes me smile. He and mom were returning home from an evening out at the same time my first love, Brent, was dropping me off. I didn't know they had followed us home and were parked directly behind us as we sat parked in front of the house kissing good-bye. When we failed to notice them after a couple of minutes, dad decided to get out of his car. He walked right out in front of us, knocked on our window, waved, and made a funny face before following my mother inside. I was so embarrassed; I gave him shit when I got in! He just laughed in his good-natured way. Mom was quick to remind me that *most* fathers wouldn't have reacted so well to their daughter necking with some guy in front of the house. I had to admit, she had a valid point.

A month or two into my first semester of Grade 11, my dad took a two-week leave of absence from work. Mom told me he'd experienced side effects from one of the medications he was on and had been to see his physician for tests. At the time, it all seemed innocent enough — he seemed his healthy, contented self — so it didn't occur to me for even a minute that he was relapsing into depression.

Two weeks turned into two months, and before long, the strain of five years past hovered over our home again. Dad was in and out of hospital, and was always prescribed a different drug each time, it seemed. None of them ever did the trick. Mom was exhausted every day when she got home from work, not so much from the day itself, but from the anticipation of caring for dad at night. He'd become a child: she had to make sure he ate and bathed or he'd forget to do it himself; if he wasn't sitting in his rocking chair rolling cigarettes in an introverted trance, he was asleep in his bed, hidden away from the outside world.

I can recall a night when I was getting ready to go out with some friends. My mom came into my room and told me that I couldn't take the car. Being the self-centred, hormone-driven teenager I was, I threw a tantrum because I thought I was being punished for something. Exhausted and frustrated, she explained to me that it was dad she was trying to put at ease. "Just wait until I get him to the hospital before you go," she pleaded. "He's afraid someone is going to trace your license and try to kill you." He wouldn't even let mom drive their own car to the hospital that night. He made her call a cab because, in his mind, that was safer.

Whichever drug had caused his paranoia was soon replaced by another, and he changed from suspicious to deeply depressed. It seemed that this time, the doctors couldn't find that special combination of meds. He slipped deeper and deeper into darkness until there was nothing left of the man we lovingly referred to as "Abby." (This was a childhood nickname that stuck throughout his life simply because it made him blush. He didn't like it, preferring his given name of Albert.)

There was an occasion when mom was at work and dad was allowed a day of leave from the hospital. My brother Michael picked him up and brought him home, but then had to leave shortly after. So, it was just me and my dad. That's when he asked me for the car keys. I shuddered. What if I gave him the keys and he didn't come back? I'd never forgive myself for letting him go. And yet, they were his keys; it was his car. It was not my place to say no.

I reluctantly gave him the keys, pacing the living room once he had left for what seemed the longest twenty minutes of my life. He returned with a bottle of whiskey from the liquor store. I was relieved knowing that at least his instinct was to come home. I was even more relieved when he returned to the hospital the next day but that relief was to be short lived. A month or two later, he was back home for good.

In my mind, it was going to be just as it had been when I was eleven years old. I knew he was suicidal, but I also believed he would recover — why else would they have let him out of the hospital? So, on that hot day in May when I asked him how he was feeling and he said, "Not so good, not so bad," I believed him. I finished my lunch, bummed a cigarette from him, and drove back to school for afternoon classes.

Mom was at work on a twelve-hour shift and wouldn't be home until eight o'clock that evening. She had asked me to make dad's supper when I got home from school knowing that otherwise he wouldn't eat at all. It was around half past three when I walked through the door. It was deathly quiet in the house. I called out for dad. When there was no answer, I started looking in all the rooms. But he was nowhere to be found.

My first instinct was to check his meds. They were in the kitchen cupboard, as usual, all the bottles full — *thank God*. "Dad?" I called again. Where was he?

I ran out to the back, and as I approached the garage door and reached for the handle, something occurred to me. We had three vehicles: one was at work with mom, Michael had taken the second one up north to camp, and I'd taken the other one to school before parking it out front at home. Relieved by the fact that there was no way he could have gassed himself, I went back into the house again.

He must be at the bar, I reasoned. He drank when he was depressed. Either that or he was at another doctor's appointment I'd forgotten about. I thought about calling mom at work but didn't want to worry her needlessly; instead, I went downstairs to my room, disappeared into my own little world, my ghetto-blaster blaring in the background.

It was half past eight when I heard mom shriek my name. That's when I knew … mom always parked her car in the garage. Sick in the very pit of my stomach at the truth I was about to learn, I flew out of my room to the foot of the stairs and faced my mother who was looking down, a terrified expression on her face. "Dad shot himself!"

"Is he dead?" was all I could say.

"No. He's still breathing." As I walked up the stairs toward her, the bottoms of my feet were on pins and needles. Soon, the numbness moved through me, consuming my entire body. Mom reached out and took me in her arms. "You and the boys are all I have left of him now," she cried, holding me so close that it was difficult to breathe. I couldn't respond. All I kept thinking as I clutched her arms was that I didn't know he had a gun.

Everything changed at that precise moment. Everything. Right down to the last detail, right down to the way things tasted and smelled. Everything changed.

One moment, I was standing in the doorway of the garage staring at squirts of blood on dad's shirt. The next, my mother and I were sitting at the kitchen table with a police officer, giving him a statement. When asked, mom couldn't even remember her own birthday. As the officer escorted us to his car outside, I saw a few other policemen taking pictures inside the garage. The next thing I knew, we were sitting in a small, white room at the emergency ward and a doctor was giving us a detailed account of how the bullet from dad's .22 calibre rifle had entered his head between his eyes, exiting through the top of his skull. I was shaking uncontrollably, but felt no emotion whatsoever. I just watched the doctor's mouth as he spoke, unable to believe a word I was hearing.

I don't know how the news travelled so fast, but it did. Soon, our home was swelling with relatives and well-wishers. Mom kept herself busy doing dishes and preparing snacks for everyone, and assigned various chores to me. Finally, I couldn't take it anymore and angrily announced, "We're the ones who lost someone here! Let them make their own damn lunches!" Mom sighed and shook her head, not about to make a scene in front of everyone. I slammed my dish towel on the cupboard and stormed down the stairs to my bedroom.

Michael returned home within twenty-four hours of receiving the news. Alex followed soon after. Both had been to the hospital to see dad for themselves, and they warned me not to go. I sat on the couch in the living room, completely numb to my surroundings. Michael broke into tears on the chair across from me. The whole scene was so surreal — like some terrible hallucination — so I decided to give myself a reality check by going back to the scene of the shooting. The blood had been scrubbed clean; not even a faint stain remained on the floor of the garage. This left me with no other alternative but to see my father for myself.

Alex drove me to the hospital the next day. I wanted to drive by myself but he refused to give me the keys. He was concerned that I'd have an accident in my agitated state, so, after a few minutes arguing, I finally gave in. It wasn't until the elevator doors opened to the floor of my father's ward that I felt my heart rate increase. Alex walked me to the entrance of dad's room and took a seat outside, giving me an opportunity to be alone with him.

There was a bed straight ahead of me when I first entered the room. Naturally, it was the one I approached.

When I took a closer look and realized it held a stranger, my eyes shifted to the right. There my dad lay, propped slightly on his right side, facing the far wall. I had to move a bit closer to get a full view of his face. At first glance, I shivered and stopped in my tracks. I almost walked right out the door. But then what would I tell Alex? I didn't want to go back out there so soon. Instead, I took a deep breath, and walked around to the other side of his bed.

I'd never seen such dark purple and black bruises in all my life. His forehead and eyes were so swollen that they had to tape his eyelids to be keep them shut. They'd also removed his false teeth, causing his jaw to sink in, making his face look even more deformed. The top of his head was completely shaven. There were bandages over the entry and exit wounds and an endo-tracheal tube in his mouth. If it were not for the fact that his chest moved up and down, I wouldn't have believed he was still alive.

It was hard to believe that it was dad laying there, so I checked his left index finger for a familiar scar; he'd cut the tip off in his workshop years ago, so when the nail grew back in, it was thick, hard, and deformed. Sure enough, it was dad. I stroked the tip of his finger. His hands were cold but his chest was warm. I placed my hand on his chest as I talked to him, hoping he might hear and feel me. I told him I was there with him and he was going to be fine — just like they do in those hospital dramas on television. It certainly felt like a hospital drama on television.

That night, I sat with my mom and brothers. We talked from half past eleven straight through until two o'clock in the morning. We discussed how calm we all were, almost relieved in a way, now that he'd finally gone through with it. There was no longer the strain of wondering when, how, and where he was going to do it. It had been done. Dad was unconscious, but breathing on his own. He was paralysed, and still clinging to life. The doctors felt that it was only a matter of time, so we made a family decision to refrain from performing any heroics and to keep him comfortable until the end.

Two weeks passed and dad was still holding on. He was starting to show some positive signs that he might come out of the coma. In the beginning, the nurses had to suction out his stomach and lungs but, after awhile, he started coughing the garbage up into the tubes himself. The doctors told us he also had pain reflexes in his arms and legs. He was able to squeeze their hands with his left hand on request.

Around this time, surgeons performed a tracheotomy on dad and removed the endo-tracheal tube from his mouth. This had to be done within two weeks or he would suffer permanent damage to the inside of his throat. The precarious procedure almost claimed his life, once again, as he suffered a blood clot in his lung four hours after surgery. His doctors kept close tabs on him through the night, but, once again, despite all the odds against him, he survived and there was a glimmer of hope.

The first time I saw dad once he'd come out of the coma, he had a huge smile on his face. Pretty ironic that it took a bullet through his head to cure his depression after all those anti-depressants he had tried. It got easier and easier to see him as the bruising started to fade and the swelling went down. Other than the fact that he had no teeth and one of his eyes was now set a bit lower than the other, he started to resemble my dad again. He couldn't talk because of the trache, but showed what seemed to be appropriate emotion, such as crying when the nurses told him it was Father's Day and laughing when we told him jokes.

The day finally came when the doctors removed the trache. After months of waiting for the inevitable suicide attempt, followed by just over two weeks of waiting for him to come out of his coma, we now restlessly waited for his neck to heal. This would determine whether or not he would be able to speak again. Well, he did. It was nothing significant, but enough to give us hope. Even the doctors who warned of a fatal aneurysm or other possible complications were amazed by his progress.

One morning, not long after the trache was removed, it happened. A nurse had just finished turning dad and asked him if he was comfortable. He responded with a hoarsely whispered, "Yep," prompting the doctors to action. They decided that perhaps surgery was in order to help improve his chances of recovery.

Now that we were older, mom was good about explaining things to us on our level whenever dad's condition changed. She came home that night after visiting him at the hospital, sat us down, and told us what we could expect next. On the day the bullet had entered my father's head, he'd developed hydrocephaly. The doctors felt that the pressure of this excess fluid on his brain impeded his ability to speak. They wanted to perform a spinal tap to drain the fluid with the hope his condition would improve. We were assured it was a safe procedure because he did not have to be put under with anaesthetic. The worst-case scenario would be that he would remain the same. We all agreed we had to at least try.

It was such an emotional time for us all. Even the doctors seemed caught up in the enthusiasm and they were already planning ahead. In the event the spinal tap improved his condition, they wanted to perform a second surgery to insert a shunt into his brain. The shunt would have a tube extending down into his abdominal cavity and act as a permanent drain. There was talk of physiotherapy and speech therapy, and the more they talked, the higher our hopes were raised. All of a sudden, it seemed everyone around us had stories to tell about scientific research that suggests the brain is capable of regenerating itself. I listened with hope when they spoke about similar patients who had recovered to live normal, healthy lives.

Not long after the spinal tap was performed, I was at home watching television in the living room. I heard

steps at the back porch and, knowing it was mom
returning from the hospital, I made my way to the door
to greet her. She happily hugged me and told me that
dad had spoken to my brother Michael that day. The
nurses told her he had been talking off and on all day!
She joined me in the living room and I was so
exhilarated by her enthusiasm; I hung on her every
word. She said that during Michael's visit, he'd asked
dad how he was feeling. Dad answered in a low whisper,
"I'm feeling fine."

I learned the term "cautious optimism" not long after
that episode. Within hours of receiving news that dad's
condition had improved, we were informed that his
temperature had gone up — and our hopes plummeted.
We were told that he had bacteria in his brain that had
been dormant since the day he shot himself, caused by
him laying in the dirt for so many hours before he was
found. The spinal tap procedure had irritated this
condition and dad was diagnosed shortly thereafter with
bacterial spinal meningitis.

In the days following, he became progressively worse.
He also contracted pneumonia in his left lung, which was
spreading to his right. Once again, mom sat us kids
down at home and gave us the same speech she'd given
after the initial attempt: she didn't want any heroics
performed, and we should let the illness take its course.
If they were to medicate him, he could survive, but he'd
inevitably suffer another complication later on. Instead,
she wanted him to be kept comfortable until the end so
that his suffering would be minimized.

I visited my father shortly after that. I could barely
breathe myself as I watched him struggle with each
shallow breath. After spending five minutes there, I
couldn't bare to see him like that anymore, so I left my
mother sobbing at his side and recklessly sped home in
my car.

That's when the anger set in. The doctors were all
incompetent, God no longer existed, and none of my

friends understood me! What kind of nightmare existence was this? What did my family ever do to deserve this? *How could we have been misled in this way and given such hope when now we were right back at square one?*

The doctors said that this complication would kill him in a week. They said that even an otherwise healthy individual treated with medication would have to battle to survive. Five days later, he defied their predictions and began recovering from the setback completely on his own. This made me stop and think. Did he really want to end his life or were all those hormones and chemicals inside him warping his mind? Surely, he couldn't have survived complications like meningitis and pneumonia without a strong will to live. It was mind-boggling.

Eventually, dad was transported from the trauma centre in the city back to the hospital in our hometown, Lanigan. Although he'd received exceptional care in Saskatoon, we all agreed our friends at home would give him that extra special touch. There was always the threat of complications looming in the background, the occasional high fever, and times he wasn't as responsive as others, but dad seemed to stabilize over the next couple of years. He learned to feed himself with his left hand, holding glasses of milk or pieces of bread by himself. He never spoke again in our presence, remained paralysed in his right arm and both legs, but he always greeted us with a smile whenever we visited.

I think the biggest smile I ever saw was when I brought my infant son, Calvin, to visit him for the first time. Whatever concern dad's eyes may have shown months before — when I told him the father was out of the picture — no longer existed. This was his first grandson. He'd lived to meet him. You could see what a gift this was by the glimmer in his eyes.

As comforting as it was to be able to see "Abby" at our convenience, it was equally exhausting to ride the roller coaster of his life. We wondered whether or not the next wave would kill him or if he'd live in this state for years to come. It was difficult to move forward without closure of any kind.

And then, about four and a half years after his suicide attempt, dad experienced divine intervention marking the beginning of the end. While being lifted from his bed into a wheelchair by a hoist, one of the straps broke and he dropped to the floor, bumping his head. The impact caused the bones in his skull to shift slightly, leaving a gap in his forehead where the excess cerebral fluid collected. With time, the pressure from that liquid stretched the skin between his eyes until it bubbled out like a huge cyst. Back then, it was horrifying for everyone involved, but, in hindsight, it was meant to be. It was time.

Over the next year, dad suffered an increase in seizures and high fevers. In a last-ditch attempt to save his life, his doctors again discussed the possibility of a shunt. There was also talk of a more elaborate procedure whereby his specialist would make an incision between his eyes and graft a piece of bone from his hip over the fracture. It was a risky operation requiring anaesthetic, so after months of discussions and debates between my mother and dad's doctors, it was finally decided to let nature take its course. They felt surgery would only cause him even more discomfort without improving his quality of life in any way.

The last time I saw dad alive, he was propped up in his special chair in the television room of the hospital. Mom was sitting beside him, holding his hand, tears in her eyes. He was too weak to lift his head anymore. It was bent forward, his chin resting on his chest. No smiles. No response. His eyes were open but he stared blankly at the floor, the pocket of fluid between them protruding even worse than before. Mom managed to spoon-feed him most of his lunch until he seizured, causing his head to move up and his whole body to constrict. He gasped for air like a woman in labour. All we could do was hold his hands and verbally comfort him. Forty seconds later, it was over. His head moved down again, his chin resting on his chest. And then no response.

When I left dad that day, I kissed him and told him I loved him. I knew it would be the last time. After years of highs and lows, victories and defeats, I just wanted him to go. I just wanted it all to end — for him *and* for the rest of us. As I watched him fall deeper into his final coma, I recalled the once patient, skilful carpenter who had built my roll-top desk from scratch. An unrelenting illness and a split-second reaction had wiped all of that away forever.

Aunt Linda, mom, and my two brothers were with dad when he died. But I chose to stay home with my two-year-old son, Calvin. I'd seen too many things over the years; I didn't want to watch him die, too. Even more, I didn't want to see the tears in my family's eyes and I didn't want them to see mine. It was just too difficult at that time.

My brother Alex phoned me with the news at five minutes to eight that October evening. I broke into tears initially, but they stopped a minute later. I had a feeling of loss and gain: losing my dad and gaining my freedom. It was over. It was finally over.

And then I smiled. I looked up toward the sky. I wondered where he was at that precise moment, if he was in the tunnel yet or had reached the light. There was something so fascinating about the fact that someone I knew and loved was experiencing the ultimate journey right then.

There are people in this world who have been pronounced clinically dead for a minute or more and then recover. When relating their experience, they talk about brilliant colours, soothing music, and a sense of understanding the universe. There are others who believe the colours, the music, the entire sensation is not life after death, but rather, a chemical in the brain that simulates the experience as it dies. Either way, it must be incredible. Whether chemical or supernatural, it's obviously not painful. That thought was very comforting for me because I realized my dad was finally free. And so were we.

I was not looking forward to the funeral service, expecting a taxing afternoon of more tears and misery. What I saw, instead, was a man peacefully asleep who looked more like my father than he had in years. I expected well-meaning friends to console us by condemning him for what he'd done, but instead I learned that many of them had visited him regularly through the years. There was such peace among us for the first time in so long. We weren't discussing his failing health but sharing stories of better times. It was clear to me that all those years of uncertainty following dad's suicide attempt were not the unfair punishment they had seemed. They were a gift of time for us to heal and reconcile with him so that when he did go, we would be able to move on with our lives gracefully. I know in my heart "Abby" was able to move on with his, too.

Karma

"*How* much money do you think you can make here?" Mr. Janzen leaned forward on the giant mahogany desk in front of him, his hands pressed together, resting on a scribbled desk calendar. He watched the unsuspecting, young woman in front of him.

I scanned the office before me. The wall behind Mr. Janzen was an array of plaques: some, awards for top sales, others, engraved reminders to strive for success. A portrait on the side caught my eye straightaway, its black border framed a barren lake of blue where a single drop of water rippled out across the page into larger and larger circles. The caption below read: *ATTITUDE is A Little Thing that Makes A Big Difference.* On the wall to my right, a long set of antlers extended toward me from the top of an elk's mammoth head. Two gaunt, polished eyes stared blankly across the room at a towering library of books.

"Well," I cleared my throat and thought about it for a moment. "I would like $1,200 a month to begin with," adding, "and once my three-month probationary period is up — "

Mr. Janzen roared with laughter, spooking me back in my chair. "I'm not talking about a measly salary, dear. I'm talking about *you*. What are *you* worth, sweetheart?"

"Well, I — " I stopped, not certain of the protocol of the situation.

Mr. Janzen rose from his plush, swivel armchair and advanced to my side of the desk. I rose obediently, maintaining eye contact with my potential employer. "Let me show you something," he said, firmly gripping my shoulder. He led me out of the office and past the reception area where I had waited for my interview earlier. "Hold my calls, Shirley," he instructed his receptionist. The woman smiled, nodded, and returned to her phone conversation.

Mr. Janzen brought me into the company boardroom and closed the door behind us. He gestured for me to take a seat at one end of the long table then went to the other end where an overhead projector faced an ivory wall. He dimmed the lights and turned it on. A chart of numbers and percentages appeared on the wall. I squinted to improve my focus.

"Now, forget about that salary for just a moment," Mr. Janzen proposed. "I'm not saying we won't offer one if that's what you prefer, honey, but humour me for a moment, will you? Let's take a look at your potential with commission. Let me show you the kind of money you can make with Janzen Block and Associates ... "

An emotional half hour of dollars and cents followed. I watched eagerly as several sheets with colourful graphs and formulas for success were flashed before me. It wasn't long before I could predict the outcomes of each scenario Mr. Janzen proposed. I began to see my true potential, just as he'd promised.

"So, what you're saying," I reiterated, "is that if I book you just five appointments, my gross income will increase by fifteen percent."

"Yes."

"And then for every additional two appointments I book on top of that five, the percentage will increase by ten percent."

"Yes."

"But I'm guaranteed minimum wage regardless of my sales."

"Yes."

I inhaled deeply and considered my options momentarily. It was a risk. I knew minimum wage would be a real financial strain; still, I liked the idea of being paid according to applied effort. It certainly beat waiting tables or sitting in some hotel gift shop for eight hours each day, as I'd been doing since graduating high school. After everything that had happened with my dad over the last three years, my mom certainly couldn't afford to put me through university. With this job, it seemed entirely possible to make a really good living, finally save up enough money for tuition all on my own. Hell, if things worked out, maybe I wouldn't even *have* to go back to school. Maybe journalism never was in the cards. "All right then," I finally answered. I had to at least try.

Mr. Janzen glowed, patting my back approvingly. "I knew you weren't a wimp. I'll see you tomorrow."

We returned to the reception area where a group of people milled around near the front desk, chatting and drinking coffee. "Hey, hey! Roger!" Mr. Janzen exclaimed, leaving me behind to join the others. The group was loud, rumbling the office with laughter and lively discourse. Amid the commotion, they did not notice me slip on my coat and exit the building.

* * *

I was anxious to prove myself, recalling the dictum about "Attitude" on Mr. Janzen's wall. I returned to the office early the next morning, ten minutes before my shift was to begin. The receptionist, Shirley, greeted me with a smile and I stood before her quietly, pacing to avoid the uncomfortable silence that seemed to hover.

"Can I help you with something?" Shirley offered after a few minutes had passed.

"I'm waiting for Mr. Janzen."

"Oh, he's out on business this morning," she informed me. "I don't expect him back until this afternoon."

I was puzzled. I had expected to meet with him that morning to review the particulars of my job. "Well, did he mention anything to you about my new position here?"

Shirley was quiet, her lips pursed together; her eyes shifted to the left as she searched her memory. At last, relief returned to her face, and she reached for a pile of sheets and a phone book on top of the counter. "Oh yes," she said. "Come with me." She escorted me to a tiny office at the end of a long, narrow hallway and presented me with the supplies in her hand. "He left these for you. You can work in here." Shirley returned to the front, leaving me alone in the room.

My office contained an armchair and a desk, empty except for a cup of pencils and a telephone. I set the phone book down and leafed through the additional sheets I'd been given: a script to guide me through phone conversations and a copy of Mr. Janzen's schedule for the month. Nothing booked for this morning, I thought to myself. I wondered where Mr. Janzen was. It all seemed a bit intimidating — my first day on the job and first real office job. I'd hoped for a bit more guidance to help me on my way. Maybe he's testing me to see how well I work independently, I reasoned. That was probably it.

I sat at the desk, flipping through the phone book from front to back before returning to the first page of numbers. My left index finger marked the first company, AAAA Bob's Butcher, while I dialed the phone with my right. I held the receiver up to my ear and listened timidly.

"Oh, yes hello," I responded. "I was wondering if the manager is available ... Katie Wright ... Janzen Block and Associates ... Yes, thank you." I waited, tracing the outline of the calendar in front of me with a freshly sharpened pencil I'd found in the cup. "Yes, hello. My name is Katie Wright and I'm with Janzen Block and Associates. Can I take a moment of your time to discuss a disability insurance package available to your company through our firm? ... Yes, but ... Yes. Thank you for your time." I hung up the phone, but my heart raced on so I stopped for a moment to compose myself. I scanned the page in front of me for a more likely candidate, then made a second attempt. "Yes, good morning. My name is Katlyn Wright. May I converse briefly with your manager, please? ... Disability insurance ... Thank you for your time."

I slammed down the receiver and swept the phone book closed with my palm, resting my elbows against the desktop, supporting my chin on folded hands. I stopped for a moment to daydream, staring at the empty wall ahead. A man like Mr. Janzen with his three-piece suits and modern office right downtown *must* know what he's talking about when he talks sales and commissions. All of his employees dressed so professionally for their surroundings. Obviously, they could afford to. Some day I would, too.

I was tired of scraping by every month. There had to be more to life. This was my first crack at making some real money and the first job that might actually lead to bigger and better things. Maybe I could be one of Mr. Janzen's agents some day. The thought warmed me and I smiled.

I knew what I had to do. Seven appointments was all it would take to earn the income I'd originally requested. Each one above that would be a sweet gratuity — extra money to set aside in savings, maybe even enough to buy my own car. Yes, I could do it! With four days left in the week, it meant only two appointments each day: one in the morning and one in the afternoon. Not so impossible really.

I reopened the phone book, flipped through its pages and returned to where I'd left off, my voice filled with renewed optimism. "Hello, my name is Katlyn Wright and I'm with Janzen Block here in town. Is your manager available? ... Yes, I'll hold."

* * *

The morning lasted forever. Three hours and thirty-seven phone calls later, it was time for my lunch break. I left my desk as it was — phone book opened and marked where I'd left off, a list of call-backs beside — and returned to the front reception area to retrieve my coat. Shirley lunched at her desk, sipping tea and nibbling a muffin.

"Any good restaurants around here?" I asked, slipping my arm into the sleeve of my worn trench coat.

"There's Kelly's Diner on the corner." Shirley brushed a crumb from her chin. She cupped a hand over her mouth, finished chewing, and swallowed. "How's it going so far?"

I raised my arms in resignation.

Our conversation was interrupted by Mr. Janzen's unmistakable throaty laughter as he drew closer to the entrance outside. I turned to face him, his left hand propping the door open. "We'll talk!" he called to a waiting Mercedes then smiled when his eyes met mine. "Katlyn!" He breezed past me. "How's day one?"

I followed him into his office like a hungry puppy expecting a treat. "Do you have a moment for me?" I asked.

"Of course." He settled in his chair. "Anything wrong?"

"Oh, no. *No.*" My head shook back and forth vigorously. "I've just come across a few objections and I'd like to run them past you. I have the list at my desk. I can get it now if you have the time." Mr. Janzen nodded and smiled so I quickly slipped out of the room, returning in a flash with my notes.

He was on the phone when I walked in. "That's right ... Uh-huh, Uh-huh ... yes ... " I stood there twiddling my thumbs until he finally acknowledged me, motioning for me to hand him my sheets. He glanced at them, but it was clear that his attention was elsewhere, so I waved and smiled, taking slow backward steps toward the door. "Yeah, hang on a minute," he told his caller. "We'll do this another time," he said to me.

"Sure," I said. I closed the door behind me.

* * *

The next two days resembled the first: endless dialing and redialing, conversations with less than obliging, protective secretaries leery of my intentions, sales pitch after sales pitch to ambivalent managers. Only two meetings had been confirmed. My first payday was just over a week away. Without five appointments, my cheque would barely cover my rent and bills, let alone extras.

Shirley was at her desk at the front when I left my office for a short breather. Shirley was always at her desk at the front, welcoming visitors into the building, directing and trafficking on Mr. Janzen's behalf.

I approached her. "I've been thinking ... "

"Yes?" She continued filing sheets of paper in the small cabinet beside her, preoccupied with the task.

"Maybe part of the problem is that I'm not familiar enough with some of the policies offered through Janzen Block, so I can't properly field people's questions. Mr. Janzen didn't really take the time to ... "

"Mr. Janzen is a busy man," Shirley retorted. She glared at me now.

"I realize that," I raised my hand in retreat, "but ... "

"You have to take the initiative in this industry," Shirley scolded. "Go to the back, find some leave-behinds, read them, and learn for yourself."

"Yes, thank you," I said. I returned to my office at the back, along the way picking up some brochures from a magazine rack on the wall. I removed my coat, hung it over the back of my chair, and sat down to read. Only moments later, it was obvious. This doesn't tell me anything, I thought. I threw the sheets down and began rubbing my temples vigorously.

I could not understand how any of these brochures were supposed to serve me. There was nothing in them explaining the details of the various policies offered through Janzen Block. They were nothing but fancy spiels intended to pique the interest of clients. They were stories, predictions, comparing the lives of two fictitious companies: one with insurance and the other without.

I thought about returning to the front room to ask Shirley if I was mistaken. Maybe these were not the brochures she had meant for me to use. If she wasn't busy, she might take the time to help; she seemed pleasant enough when relaxed. If, on the other hand, she was inundated with important business or clients, she would probably resent the interruption and abruptly send me on my way as she'd done moments ago. The thought of it was morally degrading, so I decided to stay put and make the most of the information I had.

* * *

Thursday afternoon, I stepped out of my office and walked to the back to the kitchenette. I poured myself a cup of coffee and sat down for a short break. Two other agents sat at the table ahead of me, their backs toward me. As I sat, quietly leafing through an outdated business magazine, I couldn't help overhearing their conversation.

"He's content with the coverage he has," the first man said. It was an argument I'd heard all too often.

"Did you tell him that he can opt out of workers' compensation?" the other asked. She pulled a stack of sheets from her briefcase and spread them out on the table. "For starters, workers' comp only covers accidents on the job. We can custom tailor a package, covering injury *and* illness for up to sixty percent of their income. And our coverage is guaranteed. We can freeze their premiums at the original level for as long as they have the insurance ... "

I smiled to myself. Finally, an answer! So many clients had given me the same excuse and I'd had no way to counter their objections; I'd given up on so many appointments that I may have been able to book. With my newfound knowledge and a renewed sense of confidence, I was back in my office, calling all my lost prospects back.

"Yes, hello. This is Katlyn Wright calling back. I called you earlier this morning ... Yes, yes, that's right. Listen, I've been going through some of our files here and it has come to my attention that you can opt out of worker's compensation if you are in need of more coverage ... No, there's no obligation whatsoever. And the appointment will only take about half an hour of your time. We'd just like the opportunity to show you how our plan compares to your current benefits ... Well, how's Monday morning at ten? ... Great! I'll pencil you in. Mr. Janzen will be there at ten o'clock sharp ... Great talking to you again. Bye." I hung up the phone. "Yes!"

* * *

With each phone call I made, my telephone persona became more polished, but my ignorance of the industry made selling next to impossible. The following Tuesday, I had only three confirmed appointments.

Through a crack in his door, I saw Mr. Janzen in his office on the phone. I knocked gently before entering. He pointed to the seat across from him and winked. I sat quietly with a notebook in my lap, a pen perched in my hand.

"Okay," he spoke cheerfully upon finishing his call. "How can I help you, young lady?"

"Well," I hesitated. I wanted his help without jeopardizing my position or letting him see my frustration. "I was wondering if you've had the time to look over my objections list."

"Well, let's have a look at it now," he said, flipping through the piles of paper on his desk, trying to locate the list. "You know," he spoke while continuing the search, "that retail lead you got me is a strong one. I'm confidant we'll be closing the deal this week, as a matter of fact."

That was the first positive feedback I'd heard since starting the job. "That's wonderful news," I said, feeling somewhat relieved.

Of course, his intercom buzzed. If it wasn't the intercom, it would have been the phone. "Hold on a minute," he assured me with a friendly wink. He was soon immersed in yet another conversation and I left the room, dissatisfied again.

It must have been written all over my face as I left his office and passed Shirley's desk. "What's the matter?" she asked.

I leaned against the counter and sighed: "I just don't know, Shirley."

She cocked her head sympathetically. "Give it some time," she assured me and sipped the last of her tea. "Some people are just slow learners."

I flinched, stunned. *Slow learner?*

With that, she rose from her chair, casually lifting her cup and plate. She walked around the front of her desk, on her way to the office kitchenette.

"Well, I guess I'll see you after lunch," I stammered, my face hot and flushed. Shirley nodded and smiled, then disappeared down the hall.

* * *

I sat for a long time at Kelly's Diner, brooding over my coffee, stirring it mindlessly. Occasionally, a waitress would come by offering a refill, and I would acknowledge by lifting the cup to her level or raising my hand to decline. The rest of the time, I just stared ahead, nursing my coffee, watching passers-by through the window as they hurried along in all directions. *Slow learner ... slow learner* repeated inside my head. I didn't have much experience to tell me otherwise, so who knew? Maybe I was.

I thought about a lot of things that afternoon: about my brothers, Michael and Alex, and how they'd both completed degrees in university by now. Michael, the "left brain" of the family, was strong in computer science, and was now working as a computer programmer. Alex was our "right brain" musician/language teacher who'd studied hard to become bilingual and was now teaching English as A Second Language to adults. I secretly envied them both for their brains. I'd never really applied myself in high school like they had. I'd spent far too much time socializing and not nearly enough time cracking the books. Now I was paying for it.

But I could change that, couldn't I? I was still young. It wasn't too late.

It was time to return to the office. Before leaving the restaurant, I reached into my purse for a handful of change, sorting through the pennies, dimes, and nickels, and taking two loonies from the stash. A waitress was already wiping down my table for the next customer as I stood up to leave. I tossed the change on her tray and began the trek back to the office.

* * *

Friday morning came too soon. With only five appointments booked and two more needed to earn my original requirement, I persisted. "Hi, I'm calling for Ms. Friesen. I spoke to her earlier this week … Katlyn Wright." I drummed my fingers on the surface of the desk, watching the clock on the wall ahead. It was half past eleven. "… Yes, Ms. Friesen?" I assumed a more formal posture and glanced at the notes in front of me. "Have you had a chance to review your schedule? … And which of those times is most convenient?" My heart pounded as I turned to the calendar in front of me, pointing at the prospective time slots with the tip of my pencil. "Next Tuesday at ten." I exhaled, smiling.

Shirley appeared in the doorway holding a small letterhead envelope. She waited for me to wrap up the call before entering my office.

"I did it!" I rejoiced. "Only one more now!" I picked up the receiver, eagerly punching in the next set of numbers, my adrenalin surging. Shirley advanced to the front of the desk and set the envelope down in front of me. She turned to leave me alone with my calls but was halted by my voice. "What's this?" I asked, setting the phone down, slitting the envelope open with my thumbnail. Shirley stood in the doorway watching as I pulled out my first pay cheque. "What?" The colour drained from my face.

"Payroll is done the *morning* of the fifteenth, Katie."

"But I was told ... "

"You were told payroll is done twice monthly. Did you think I would hold up everyone else's cheques until ten minutes to five on your account?" she jeered, her eyebrow raised. She left me alone, closing the door behind her.

I was one sale away. One sale away! I held the cheque at face level, both hands gripping either end. I turned it over and back, examining both sides, not looking for anything in particular. I took a fleeting look at the figure on the cheque. When the amount registered moments later, I peered at it again, pulling a calculator from the front drawer of my desk and vigorously punching in my own calculations. "This can't be right," I reasoned aloud, and I set out to find Shirley, cheque in hand.

She was back at her desk, perched at her computer, typing from a scribbled notebook on her right. "Problem?" she quipped on my approach.

"Yes." I handed her the cheque. "I wasn't paid any commissions. I was supposed to get fifteen percent for the five appointments I've already booked."

Shirley rolled her eyes and gave the cheque back to me. "The money isn't yours until it's in the bank, dear." She returned to her position in front of the computer.

I stood behind her, thrown by her frostiness. "Where is Mr. Janzen?" I finally asked, trying with all my might to control the quivering of my voice.

Shirley faced me again, her eyes bulging out lividly. "Mr. Janzen is a busy man."

"Yes, I know. You've told me," I snapped back. I clenched the cheque tightly, inadvertently crumpling one end with my fist. "But where is he?"

Shirley began bustling about her desk, organizing papers, returning stray pens and pencils to their respective containers. "Mr. Janzen is busy with client business right now, as am *I*."

"Too busy to develop your employees?" My voice rose another octave, "Too busy to give me all the details upfront?"

Shirley crossed her arms in front. "Well, I'm sorry you feel you were misled."

I shook my head in disbelief. I couldn't speak and yet I couldn't leave, our stares locked.

"Well, if we're done here," she eventually balked, rolling her chair back toward her computer.

There was nothing left to say. I could protest until I was blue in the face; no one in that building was going to hear me. I began the route back to my office to collect my coat from the back of my chair. I hung it over my left arm, rifling through the pages on the desk with my right. I picked up my script, read the first two or three lines, then set it back down on the disordered pile.

"Give Mr. Janzen my regards," I called to Shirley as I passed the reception desk. A cool breeze rippled across the back of her blouse as the lobby door swung closed behind her.

* * *

Years later, I enjoyed better success in advertising sales with Saskatoon's daily newspaper. My department was inundated with business and unable to adequately service all the smaller clients, so a series of interviews were held to find a suitable assistant. The successful candidate, we were told, was a gentleman with ample sales experience. He had what it took to grow these accounts and build a territory of his own. My interest was piqued.

I don't know who was more surprised when we saw each other again — me or Mr. Janzen. "How are you?" I asked, shaking his hand, fighting the urge to question his current circumstance. What was he doing here?

Mr. Janzen held a stack of files. "Would you mind briefing me on each of these clients?" he asked pleasantly, now a mere shadow of the venerable man I once knew.

My phone rang. I smiled. "Just a moment," I winked at him and picked up the line. "Katlyn here ... Yes ... Uh-huh, Uh-huh ... Hold on a moment, will you?" I turned toward Mr. Janzen who sat patiently waiting for my assistance. "You know," I said, "this is probably going to take awhile. Why don't I catch up with you later?"

One Night Changed Everything

This isn't happening, this isn't happening, I rocked myself back and forth. The bus pulled into my stop, jolting me back to reality. I rose habitually, picking up my duffel bag from the seat. I felt clumsy, shuffling past all the weary passengers to the back exit, out onto the snow-packed street. I needed some time alone and wanted to hide far away from everyone. Jason would be calling soon to see how things went. How was I going to tell him?

It hardly seemed real. An hour ago, I was sitting in the doctor's office, staring at the wall and waiting for my results to come back. I was anxious to get home and get on with my day. It wasn't my regular clinic. It was farther from home, and filled with unfamiliar staff who didn't know me or my family. Once I got the test back, I thought I would never have to return. No one would have to know I'd even questioned the possibility.

I looked at my watch and anxiously exhaled. What in God's name was taking so long? I stood up and moved to the other side of the room to study a poster of disease-infested lungs for the umpteenth time. Finally, the doctor appeared and I offered her a smile, not at all anticipating the bombshell she was about to drop on me.

"Well ... " She bit her bottom lip. "Your test came back positive, Katie."

"*Positive*?" my voice quivered. My jaw dropped.

The doctor's expression was a cross between concern and disapproval. "Yes."

When I asked her exactly how far along I was, she wasn't certain. She guesstimated that I was somewhere between three to five weeks based on my recollection of my last menstruation. I couldn't believe it. I honestly didn't think I could be pregnant. The only reason I even went to the doctor that morning was for Jason's peace of mind. I was about seven or eight days late for my period, but it had been irregular in the past, so it had him more worried than me. There was no nausea, unusual bloating, or anything of the sort to prepare me for this. I really didn't think I could be pregnant.

Now, I trudged down the street to my apartment building, with so many thoughts filling my head and so many emotions clashing inside. Not only could I not think straight, but I must have dropped my keys five times while fumbling to open the mailbox. I pulled all the fliers out and leafed through them mechanically, my eyes not really registering their content. I couldn't get the doctor's voice out of my head. *Your tests came back positive, Katie … positive, Katie … positive, Katie.* I found myself terrified and amazed: one minute, feeling like death had warmed over; the next, smiling dreamily at this miracle. I was pregnant. *I* was pregnant. *Me.*

I knew exactly when it happened. It was that night at Jason's place when his roommate wasn't home, after a quiet dinner and slow dancing by candlelight. It was a warm and relaxing evening until we both realized the condom had torn. We avoided discussing it, kissing each other good night instead. But I could see the question mark in his eyes and I'm sure he could see it in mine. It wasn't brought up again until the night before my appointment at the walk-in clinic.

This was a delicate subject for any couple, let alone two people who'd only known each other for three months. We hadn't even argued yet, still enjoying the "lovey-dovey" stage of our relationship, so our conversation was sketchy and brief. Jason's restless demeanor told me that he had no interest in being a parent at twenty. My first instinct was to comfort and assure him that he had nothing to worry about. All I wanted was to get the damn pregnancy test over with so we could get back to the way things were — heavenly.

Now the pregnancy test was complete. So much for *ever* getting back to the way things were. No matter what decision we made, things would never be the same between us. I allowed a stream of tears to flow down my face once my apartment door was closed and locked. I leaned back against the door. What was I going to tell Jason when he phoned? God damn it, this wasn't happening, this wasn't happening.

I thought about all of the rumours that would soon be circulating, Jason's disappointment, and our lost freedom. I immediately thought of abortion. No one would have to know. I wouldn't have to disrupt our lives. It would be like none of this ever happened if I got rid of it right away. The thought provided temporary relief until my conscience reminded me of the strong maternal urges I'd felt during the past year. Ironically, only a month or two before, my mother and I'd met for coffee and discussed these feelings. She'd told me that it was natural for a young woman my age to have these feelings. So how could I even entertain the idea of abortion after that? Maybe this was my only chance to have a child. How could I ignore it?

I anxiously paced the length of my living room, the phone coming into view upon each turn, reminding me that there was another person involved. He would be calling soon. I pulled a tissue from my pocket and rubbed the smeared mascara from my stinging eyes. The tears didn't want to stop, my lids flooding again as soon as I wiped them dry. How was he going to react to this? Judging by yesterday's conversation, probably not well.

I worried about Jason's family the most. I'd only met them once or twice in passing, so I barely knew them at all. What I did know was that they were fairly religious, church-going people. That could work for or against us: they may very well be loving and supportive of any decisions we made; on the other hand, maybe they would disown Jason over this or force him to marry me, making our lives a living hell. Either way, the thought of facing them made me cringe with shame. It's not as though Jason and I had been together all that long. If pressed, it might be easier to explain this had we been dating for a couple of years.

My family? I wasn't thrilled about telling them — especially my very Catholic Grandma — but I knew that once the initial shock wore off, they would accept it. After everything that had happened with "Abby" over the last few years, this may even bring them some joy. This was something to look forward to for a change: a brand new edition to our family. Well, that is, if we decided to keep the baby.

A small, round cushion lay on the couch across the room. I couldn't resist stuffing it under my sweatshirt and looking into the mirror. I observed the front and side view of what would soon be my new figure. My mouth formed a smile. Then the tears came again.

What about school? I'd just been accepted into Carleton University in Ottawa for their pre-journalism program. If we kept our baby, there was no way I'd be able to go. My approximate due date was three months into the school year. That's when it really hit me — what I'd be giving up for this child. I'd have to stay in Saskatoon for at least another year and, if Jason and I got married, maybe indefinitely. Was I honestly prepared to do that?

As I stood before the mirror, it was as though I was staring at a stranger. Somehow I looked different; I felt different. My face was pale and lifeless, my eyes revealing the fear and uncertainty inside. Never before had I felt so unattractive. I wondered if Jason would still love me ... or if he ever did, for that matter.

What about adoption? This may be the greatest gift we could ever give another couple unable to have children of their own. This was a heart-warming thought, but somehow I knew I'd never be able to go through with it. The idea of giving birth to this infant after nine months of bonding with him, never seeing or knowing him, hurt as much as our other options did, if not more. This was *my* child. *My child. My child.* Kind of had a ring to it.

I cradled my lower abdomen with my hand, rubbing gently over the area. Was this baby a boy or a girl? I tried to imagine what our combined attributes would look like. Green eyes? Brown eyes? Blonde? Brunette? I sat there for a good twenty minutes, concentrating on that one detail alone, staring into space, smiling the entire time.

It's not like we were sixteen, anymore: I was nineteen; Jason was twenty. We both had our own places. We had jobs, albeit not the best paying jobs, but we'd be able to get by. This baby wouldn't go without.

I sank back into my sofa, cuddling the cushion against my chest. I closed my eyes and envisioned a fair, little girl in front of a mirror with me standing behind her, braiding her delicate, flowing hair. I peered out through sheer white drapes that blew open to a window on our right. There in the yard was a little boy, ball cap on his head, kicking a big, colourful beach ball through a sprinkler. He was running after it, getting soaked. And then I was there with him, running through the sprinkler, chasing him around the yard. No matter how hard I tried, I couldn't see their faces nor could I hear their voices. But I felt them. They felt so real for that moment and so right. Then it hit me all over again — I was pregnant. Involuntarily, I started rocking myself back and forth, back and forth. *My God, my God, my God.* What had I done? I wasn't ready for this.

My train of thought was interrupted by the phone, its jarring ring propelling me up from my seat. I knew it was Jason. I stood paralysed for another two or three rings before walking over and lifting the receiver to my ear. "Hello ... Fine. You?" I closed my eyes tight, squeezing salty tears down my cheeks. Then I told him, "We have a lot of decisions to make."

Invincible

*W*hen I decided to keep my son and raise him alone, I figured I knew what I was getting myself into. I was twenty years old and indestructible. Maybe that confidence was good in a way. It was that naïvete that kept me going for the first while. I didn't have a very good job, I held nothing more than a high school diploma, and his father was long gone. Still, I believed that would all change in a year or two. A child wasn't going to keep me from working my way up the corporate ladder, socializing with friends, and dating men. I'd seen other women do it. I could do it, too.

My child was a blessing because he was this little person who would love me unconditionally for the rest of my life. He was never going to leave me. I found that especially comforting after the events of the last few years which had left my father paralyzed in the hospital, and had completely shaken my sense of security.

Somehow, because it was my decision to raise this child alone, I had to prove to the world that I was capable and strong enough to handle it all on my own. I didn't ask for much help in the beginning — doing so would have been admitting weakness. It gave me a real sense of pride to hear friends and relatives say, "How do you do it?" or "*I* wouldn't be able to do it."

I'd always respond with, "Well, you just *do*. It's not really all that bad." And it wasn't in the beginning. I was still fresh and new. I could see the light at the end of the tunnel and knew it wasn't always going to be a struggle.

Money wasn't very good, but I learned how to get by. I knew which stores accepted post-dated cheques and the ones that didn't process them for a few days. I knew the exact dates my family allowance and GST credits would arrive. There were times when I was down to about five diapers and half a carton of milk with three days to wait until payday. Somehow, things always worked out. In a way, the experience was good for me because it taught me that no matter how bad things got, I could always survive. But after awhile, it wore on my nerves and self-esteem. I tried to hide the poverty from friends and family, not wanting them to see the empty fridge or the unpaid bills because then they'd see that I wasn't doing a good job on my own. I wasn't managing my money well enough; I wasn't providing a good enough life for my son.

With a monthly net income of only $1,100, the truth is it *was* difficult to provide a good life for my son: rent was $450; day-care was $200; diapers, formula, and baby food were $150; power was $25; phone was $50; and I spent a mere $150 on groceries each month. That left me with $75 for spending money. I hadn't even put gas in the car yet. I hadn't taken my son and I for hair cuts. How would I pay for medicine if we got sick? Or new winter clothes? Or tickets to the occasional movie without this treat cutting into my rent or phone bill? Never mind the fact that I was physically and emotionally dependent on cigarettes. It is easy to imagine how quickly I went into debt.

If it had not been for my mom, I wouldn't even have had a car. When she learned I was pregnant, she scraped together enough money to buy me a 1980 Mercury Zephyr, so I wouldn't have to sit at the bus stop with an infant in frigid weather during the winter months. I remember so many times driving home after work with the gas gauge teetering on empty, chanting, "Please, just get me home! Please, just get me home!" until I was safely parked in my stall. Payday was still a day away and gas stations were onto people like me, so they no longer accepted personal cheques.

There was no way I could afford car repairs. My daily ritual began with the same prayer: Dear God. Please let the car start today. Amen. I'd get my son all bundled up in his car seat, then hold the gas peddle to the floor and turn the key in the ignition. On a good day, the engine would roar on the second or third try. That's when I'd pop the hood, unplug the overnight battery charger (also compliments of my mother), and flip the butterfly so it wouldn't rev so high. From there, I'd drive to the nearest gas station to fill the front, passenger-side tire with air. It had a slow leak, but I was trying to make it last as long as possible before calling mom for the money to replace it. It was degrading having to phone my mother to bail me out time and again. I didn't want to have to do it unless absolutely necessary.

I can vividly recall one particular evening, driving home from day-care with my son on Circle Drive. A man to the right of me tried changing lanes without a proper shoulder check so I honked my horn to let him know I was there. Well, the horn stayed on. All the way home. For twenty-three blocks. When I finally pulled into my stall, I managed to turn it off by jiggling the signal light switch. I exhaled and turned to face my son, Calvin, who was staring up at me, adoringly. "How about that, kiddo?" I said, brushing his blonde hair out of his eyes with my fingertip. "Feel safe, yet?" I was a very proud person who didn't want to draw any attention to my situation. Still, that was pretty difficult when I was driving around in a big, yellow lemon with black smoke trailing behind me, and a horn that announced my arrival wherever I went.

I thought about going back to school a lot. I did end up in business college for a year, which helped improve my finances somewhat. Still, I wasn't really that much further ahead because my expenses increased with the additional student loan payment. And, in turn, my day-care subsidy subsequently decreased. University was definitely out of the question after that. There was no way I'd be able to work my way through with a small child at home. I knew I'd have to finance the full four years with student loans. By the time I got out, I'd have a mortgage and no house to show for it. Not to mention the fact that I wouldn't be guaranteed a good paying job with hours similar to my son's day-care hours. Defeated, I continued to work.

It was pretty tough to climb that corporate ladder when I had another full-time job at home. It wasn't just the time and energy involved in raising my son while working full-time that wore me down, but the emotional impact. It was the guilt I felt when prying him from my leg to leave him at day-care, and the guilt when I missed work to stay home with him. There were piles of paperwork all around me at the office and mounds of laundry all around me at home. I couldn't win either way, because I couldn't give myself a break. I felt like I was letting everyone down.

The light at the end of the tunnel faded with each passing year. I watched in envy as all of my childless friends married, bought property, and moved ahead in life where I couldn't seem to. I felt so empty and inadequate with the knowledge that I'd still be renting in the foreseeable future and that my Calvin didn't have his own yard to play in.

Although the money slowly improved with promotions or new jobs, the damage was already done. I became more and more resentful. Even the simple things had become more difficult. If I ran out of milk in the evening, I had three choices: I could either bundle up my son and take him with me to the store, try to find a baby-sitter for him so I could go alone, or not go at all. Most of the time it was such a hassle, I ended up not going. It was like living in a cage. I felt so alone.

I remember one night being so exhausted that all I wanted to do was sit on the couch and read a book. That's all I wanted. My son kept approaching me with toys and puzzles but I kept turning him down. "Just half an hour to myself, please!" I announced and he disappeared into his bedroom, his little head drooping forward, his bottom lip protruding. After a time, the calm was unnerving, so I went to check on him. He had fallen asleep on his bed, still fully clothed, waiting for me to spend some time with him. I can't even begin to describe the guilt I felt *that* night — I cried myself to sleep. The next day I overcompensated with a trip to the zoo, a bike ride by the river, ice cream, and a new toy from The Dollar Store. That kid didn't know what hit him.

Dating was a whole other issue in itself. The older my son got, the more difficult dating became. Just trying to build a relationship with someone was pressure enough, let alone adding a third person to the equation. I felt bad when romantic evenings were interrupted by Calvin's perfectly normal, childish antics; I felt even worse knowing that Calvin had to endure all of the ups and downs of my relationships with me. And, as more time passed, I couldn't help but resent the freedom my dates seemed to have, being able to come and go as they pleased while I felt so confined.

Eventually finances, work, and parenting all took their toll. My energy levels drained, my desire to socialize depleted, I grew more reclusive. My sole motivation to get out of bed in the morning was knowing that I'd be able to get back into it again at night. My friends could see what was happening and would invite me out to try to get me out of this rut. I knew they were right, and I'd always start out every Monday with good intentions, agreeing to meet with them on the weekend. I promised. But, by Wednesday, I was weighing the benefits of friendship and companionship against the quiet comfort of my couch and television. And, by Friday, the couch usually won. I was spent.

What was happening to me? I no longer saw my son as the little person who would love me forever. I saw him as my sole responsibility, and that scared the hell out of me. It seemed no one else was there to help me mould him into a respectable human being. No one was there to relieve me when I needed a break. All of the decisions were mine to make, the expenses were mine to pay, and the problems were mine to solve. Some days, the pressure was unbearable.

The turning point for me came when I finally got tired of being tired. I knew something had to change or I was going to fade away. But it was figuring out what needed changing that was the greatest challenge. It took a lot of soul searching before I knew what I needed to do, to identify the three small but significant changes I needed to make.

The first and probably most important change was that I began to recognize the patterns that led to resentment and exhaustion. I learned that it was actually *more* tiring staying home weekend after weekend than it was to make time for my friends. I had to force myself to leave the house those first couple of nights, even though I knew I'd have fun once I went. Before long, I made socializing a habit again, reserving one night for friends every other weekend. What a difference it made in my attitude when I began enjoying the company of my adult friends again. The door to my cage opened wide.

Second, I learned to be less critical of myself. I stopped competing with neighbours and friends who had better cars, nicer furniture, or houses of their own. It was amazing, the tension I released from my body when I finally realized it was okay to have fewer material things right now. It would all come in time. Once I took that pressure off, a tremendous weight was lifted from my shoulders, and I gained a healthier perspective. Suddenly, I wasn't a failure anymore. I could see how successful I really was.

And last, but certainly not least — I bought a crock pot! How I survived for all those years without one, I'll never know! All the nights of macaroni and cheese, because I was too exhausted or there wasn't enough time to make a decent meal, became a thing of the past. We started eating the healthy, balanced meals we'd been lacking for so long. What a difference that made to our health and energy levels.

Parenting is a tough job even when there are two people to share it. Raising a child is not something I will ever take lightly again. If anything, I've learned a lot about my character over the last several years. I know I can be strong when I have to be but I'm by no means invincible. And there's no shame in that.

Mother Hen

Some days, I really don't think I was cut out to be a parent. I wish I could say I have that innate maternal instinct my mother was blessed with, but, to tell you the truth, it doesn't come that naturally to me. I have trouble enough managing my own affairs let alone worrying about a small child's.

When I brought my son Calvin home from the hospital for the very first time, I didn't have a clue what I was doing. As the baby of my own family, the only exposure I'd had to infants was through the odd baby-sitting job I'd taken as a young teenager. My motherly mother reassured me time and again. She said it would all come to me, just as it does to every other woman. I would know what he needed and would be able to differentiate between the "hungry cry," versus the "soiled cry," versus the "I want attention cry." Well, maybe I wasn't listening hard enough but they all sounded the same to me. There was nothing intuitive about it — it was more like hit or miss.

As an infant, Calvin's "cranky time" ranged anywhere from seven o'clock in the evening to midnight, and occasionally all the way through. He would cry and cry, and I'd be rocking him, checking his diaper, warming his bottle, patting his back, blowing him kisses, and shoving colourful squeeze toys in his face to divert his attention. When none of that worked, I'd find myself crying right along with him. It must have been quite a show for our neighbours in the apartment below.

One evening, after a tiresome three-hour marathon of tears — the kid was crying, too — it occurred to me that it might be more than the "burp, bottle or bum" that my *New Mother Manual* suggested. Did it occur to the author of that book for even a minute that maybe, just maybe the child was itchy? I get itchy once in awhile, so maybe babies do, too. And when that itch is between your shoulder blades, in that place you can't reach without a helping hand, it can be enough to make *anyone* cry.

I placed Calvin on his tummy, on a blanket, while I disappeared into the washroom to find his soft-bristled baby brush. When I returned, he was howling, his little head bobbing up and down as he searched the room for his deserter. I knew I was in for a long and sleepless night if I didn't respond to his demands — and quickly. Gently, I stroked the brush across his back. At first, it caught him off guard; he squawked defiantly. Thirty seconds later, he was cooing with relief. It was a triumphant moment for me!

As if pregnancy, labour, sleep deprivation, and the teething months weren't enough, *then* there was potty training. Potty training, I learned very quickly, was not my forte at all. But it had to be done. And, after hearing Susan from down the hall boast about having both of her twins completely trained at twenty-two months, I felt increased pressure to get the ball rolling as two years old came and went.

So, here was my first dilemma: he was a boy; I was a girl. Clearly, I couldn't demonstrate the proper male technique for him. We spent hours together, bonding in front of his miniature toilet in the bathroom. I would kneel beside my naked little boy who stood puzzled, wondering what we were doing there. I tried everything I could think of: coaching him, praising him, running the tap beside him. Not even a trickle. Well, at least, not until I brought him back down the hallway to his bedroom to put on a pair of Pull-ups. When I turned around and looked, there was often a wet, dotted trail behind us.

One day, we were out for a walk by the Saskatchewan River. It was a pastime we often enjoyed together during the warmer seasons. Wouldn't you know, when we got as far away from the car and public washrooms as we possibly could, the child decided he had to pee and, Pull-ups be damned, he wanted to try it the "big boy" way. I looked around to see if there was anyone nearby. "Come here," I said, taking his hand, leading him to a clearing behind a bush. I undid his zipper in the nick of time then helped him hold it steady so he wouldn't wet his shoes. His eyes lit up as he watched the stream in front of him. This was exciting stuff! He was starting to understand.

Later that evening, back at home, I was doing dishes when I heard Calvin call to me, "Mommy! Go pee!"

"Okay! Just a minute!" I shook the excess soap suds from my hands and grabbed a dish towel from the cupboard. To my surprise (and fright), he was not in the washroom. He was not in the hallway. He was not in his bedroom. Do you want to know where I found him? Out on the balcony, peeing over the side, on the trunk of an elm tree. It took me a couple of days to get through to him that peeing in bushes *is* acceptable, but only when there isn't a toilet nearby.

Potty training took a lot longer at my house than it did at Susan's. In the end, I don't think it was *me* who trained him at all; it was something he had to figure out for himself. I knew he finally had it mastered when he stumbled into the living room one night, his pants around his ankles, with a huge smile on his face. "Mommy, come!" he said, tugging on my arm, pulling me toward the bathroom. There, in the toilet was a perfect, little specimen. What a shame we had to flush it away. (What a shame we couldn't show it off to Susan the super mom first.)

It seems like some women in this world were born to be mothers. My mom is one of these women. I like to refer to her kind as a "mother hen." You know the type: nurturing, patient, reliable, organized. My mom had this eerie ability to hear her children turn over in bed from two rooms away in the deepest of sleeps. If my brothers and I so much as coughed at night, she would be up in an instant, fluffing our pillows, rubbing Vicks Vapour Rub on our backs, slipping a thermometer under our tongues, and filling the humidifier with water. It didn't matter if she'd just worked a twelve-hour shift at the hospital and had to get up in two hours to work another shift — we could always count on her.

Me, on the other hand … now that's a whole other story. When my son was a toddler, I used to let him sleep in the same bed with me, not so much because I was nurturing, but because I got damn tired of fighting with him to stay in his own bed once he'd graduated from the crib. Anyway, I remember one night when he rolled over next to me and prodded my back with his bony fingertip. "Mommy, I can't bweeve. My node is pwugged."

I stared at him with this half-asleep, dimwitted gaze and considered our options momentarily. "Well, open your mouth then," was all I could come up with before rolling over and falling back asleep. What can I say? It was two o'clock in the morning and I had to work the next day. It seemed like a good answer at the time.

I must admit, I secretly loathe mother hens (well, not so secretly anymore, I suppose). They always put me to shame. When they throw birthday parties for their children, everything is planned days in advance right down to the hand-painted invitations, the personalized balloons and streamers, and the homemade, double-decker, meticulously decorated "Bert and Ernie" theme cake. They seem to have Martha Stewart's time and energy (and desire, for that matter) to arrange all kinds of creative crafts for their guests to enjoy. When it's all over, each child is sent home with a neat, little gift bag filled with party favours and homemade chocolates. This, of course, is followed by a thank-you card in the mail with a group photo of all their friends enclosed.

I decided I could measure up and tried organizing this type of party for Calvin's third birthday. What a nightmare. My horror began with a series of panicked phone calls to all the day-care moms one day prior, begging them to bring their children over Saturday afternoon, bribing them with the promise of enjoying two hours of freedom while I babysat for them at no charge. From there, I did a whirlwind tour of Zellers during my lunch hour to buy my son's gift and all of the decorations, pop, and munchies I would need. On Saturday morning, I decorated the apartment, filled all the gift bags, and wrapped Calvin's present. I felt so accomplished, anxiously watching the time tick away. There was only one more hour before our guests would arrive. That's when it hit me like a half-ton truck — I'd forgotten the bloody cake!

Luckily, there was a Dairy Queen close by. Even more fortunate, that Dairy Queen had a drive-through window. "Just give me a happy birthday ice cream cake!" I called to the intercom as I fumbled through my purse for my wallet.

"Any special message on it?" a young voice answered back.

"Can you do it in five minutes?"

"Sure," she said.

"Okay, ummm … Happy Birthday Calvin!" I pulled ahead to the window in a heartbeat.

There was a lingering five-minute wait before the girl appeared with the box and handed it to me. I quickly grabbed it and set it on my son's knee beside me. He was glowing with anticipation as I paid for it and we raced home in the car. When we arrived, I opened the box. The cake said "Happy Birthday *Kevin*." Oh, what the hell, I thought. Close enough. It's not like the kid could read, anyway.

The party guests began rolling in one by one over the next half hour. I ended up with six children ranging in age from two to five, all pawing at me for attention and "Juice!" How was I going to keep them entertained for the next two hours? Then it came to me. We could all sit at the table and create pictures with glue and sparkles. It was perfect! That way, I wouldn't have to worry about them all screaming and rumbling through my home like a thunderstorm.

Note to self: never again offer preschoolers glue and sparkles to play with.

If patience had been one of my virtues, it may not have bothered me when Brandon knocked an entire jar of golden sparkles into the chips. I might have casually laughed it off when Emma set the glue bottle down on its side, letting it slowly drip onto the rug below. "Okay!" I clapped my hands together like an old school marm. "That was fun! Now let's watch Barney!" I glanced at the clock as I herded them giggling and squealing into the living room: one hour and forty-five minutes left to go.

If you've ever had the *privilege* of listening to Barney for any length of time, then you'll know what I mean when I say !@%&?!. For those of you who haven't, Barney is an annoyingly spirited, big, purple dinosaur who was all the rage when my son was three. The kids sat mesmerized by him as he danced before them on television, singing ear-piercing medleys with overly zealous children. My only reprieve during the hour-long "Barney! Live In New York!" video was that it would leave us with just enough time to eat the cake and open presents before the other parents returned to my rescue.

"Oh, they were wonderful! No problem at all!" I assured parents as they filed out my door with their children *two and a half* hours later. I stood out in the hallway calling, "Thank you! Thank you for coming!" repeatedly until the last of them disappeared around the corner. I made sure every one of them heard me loud and clear so they weren't disappointed when a thank-you card didn't follow in the mail.

Calvin sat beaming at the kitchen table amid all the half-eaten, melting pieces of cake, his own sporting the letters "Kevi" in bright pink icing. "Tangkoo, mommy," he said, hugging me. At least *someone* thought I was a star.

My stress levels only skyrocketed once Kindergarten started. Now I found myself competing with a myriad of mother hens to design contest-winning Halloween costumes and bake brownies for school events. Fortunately, Calvin was fairly easy-going and agreed to being swathed from head to toe in athletic foam underwrap for Halloween (he won "Most Original Costume" for being the only mummy in his class). Unfortunately, the whole brownie thing for the Christmas bake sale didn't go as well as planned ...

I did everything according to Betty Crocker's instructions, so I'm not sure exactly where I went wrong, but when I pulled the pan from the oven, my brownie had rock-hard edges and a bubbly, concave centre. Now I know what you're thinking. At that point, I probably should have thrown in the towel and headed straight for the nearest bakery. But this was Calvin's school bake sale. Determined to make him proud and present something "homemade" like all the other moms, I cut the brownie into squares, smoothed the tops with a thick coat of chocolate icing, and arranged them all on a foil tray.

There were deserts displayed on blanketed tables along the hallway at his school as far as the eye could see: cakes formed like trains with Oreo cookies for wheels and black liquorice connecting the cars, candy-cane sugar cookies, delectable cherry pies, and homemade tarts. When no one was looking, I removed the tinfoil wrapping from my tray and set it down toward the back of the table beside some store-bought chocolates. Store-bought chocolates, eh? I smiled. I'm not alone in this world.

I'd forgotten all about my brownies for a time, preoccupied with a group of carolling children down the hall, until I heard the painful yelp of a young boy bringing the off-key chorus of *Silent Night* to a halt. "My tooth!"

I turned to see him with his mother, her faced flushed as she consoled him on bended knee. "Oh look!" she said, trying to distract him and all the other prying eyes, "You've lost your first tooth. This is an extra special one for the tooth fairy."

"That wasn't the loose one!" he wailed, his mouth smeared with all too familiar chocolate icing. I felt myself shrinking inside.

"It's getting late," the embarrassed woman took her son by the arm, ushering him to the exit.

"But I'm not done my brownie!"

"You can finish it in the car. Let's *go*."

With a few experiences like these under my belt, I'm beginning to learn and accept my limitations as a mother. Needless to say, I don't bake for public events anymore. When those volunteer fund-raiser notices come home in Calvin's backpack, I tend to tick off the boxes for selling raffle tickets or working bingos, instead. Or, I avoid them altogether.

Of course, did the fun stop there? No! When Calvin learned how to read and write in Grade 1, I had a whole new appreciation for those earlier years. There was something disturbing about the idea that he could now communicate things about our home life to everyone in his class. I got my first taste of his creative writing while waiting my turn for parent/teacher interviews. A mosaic of paintings and compositions covered the walls outside the classroom to keep parents entertained during the delay.

"Oh, isn't that precious!" I heard another woman giggle. I glanced in her direction to see little Krista's story about her dad: *My dad likes eatting stake, watching football and reeding the paper. By Krista.* Wasn't that cute!

As I scanned the wall, I learned all kinds of things about the other parents: Michael's mom liked cheesecake and quilting; Samantha's dad loved golfing and beer. I couldn't help chuckling about the beer thing — how embarrassing for Samantha's dad! — until I came to my own son's paper, replacing my amusement with chagrin: *My mom likes craft dinner, playing Nintendo and five minits to herself pleaze. By Calvin.* There was no denying it; he hit the nail right on the head with that one.

I suppose there's something to be said for parents like me. My son is a lot more independent than I was as a child; I like to think it's because he is not as sheltered. I'm not one of those doting mothers who does everything for him, so he's mature beyond his years in many ways. How many other seven-year-olds do you know who can assemble their own electric-train set from Santa? Like *I* was even going to attempt it?

Calvin still gets that mother hen touch — Christmas baking, knitted scarves, and homemade soup — when we visit my mom and other relatives. Things will sure be different for his kids, though. We'll be ordering in pizza at my house and, if they're lucky, they might even get a gift certificate from Toys R Us.

Love Is Not Biological

*M*y romance with Scott was difficult to define, which, thinking back, is probably a lot of the reason why it ended. But the bond remained there between he and my son, Calvin, even after seven hours of highway driving separated them.

I met him through my first love, Brent, when I was turning fifteen. I thought that Scott was so perfect the first time I saw him. I couldn't take my eyes off him. I was sitting in a booth at McDonald's with Brent when he appeared before us. He was with his girlfriend, hand in hand. It was his face that caught my attention straightaway: blue eyes complemented by perfectly formed, soft brown eyebrows, a chiselled jaw line and wavy, dark brown hair. I already knew then that I would see him again after Brent moved away to Ontario with his parents.

I was quite a different person at that time: carefree, boy-crazy, shy but sociable. Twelve years later, as I stood in front of my balcony window watching for Scott's headlights to appear, the strain of adulthood weighed heavy on my shoulders. I was unhappy with us. He was unhappy with us. We had finally reached our crossroad.

It was wintertime. It was that period during all Saskatchewan winters when it's still black outside when your alarm goes off in the morning and dark again by the time you leave work to return home. When you're surrounded by that kind of darkness and cold for any length of time, it affects your moods tremendously. Everything difficult in your life seems that much more dismal, and the tasks once easy to perform in the warmer months are too much of a hassle.

When Scott's car didn't appear after several minutes, I took my seat on the couch and fumed awhile longer.

Late again. It figured. He was chronically laid back about time, while I was anal about punctuality. It was one of those small details that festered more now than ever before.

It's not that one of us was right or wrong. It's that the dynamics between us were shifting. For his part, he hadn't changed a bit since I met him. He remained the carefree bachelor, playing hockey with "the boys" twice weekly, meeting them at the bars each weekend to socialize, coming and going from his bachelor pad as he pleased. For my part, I *had* changed — and not necessarily for the better. I felt surrounded by the sorrows and ghosts of the past few years, bitter at the unfair balance between finances and responsibilities. I was envious and resentful of Scott's freedom, and uncertain where my (our?) future was headed.

We'd discussed moving in together on more than one occasion. We'd also discussed marriage. Perhaps the reason we never went through with either was because, in the back of our minds, we knew things weren't right between us. Whenever one of us was ready to move forward, the other wasn't in the same space. It was like a tug-of-war for eleven years, with too many break-ups, time-outs, and infidelities on both sides. Hardly marriage material. Even our respective families were confused by us, neither of them ever purchasing Christmas presents until late in the season, because they never knew if we'd be together that year or not. It became the ongoing joke.

But it didn't feel like a joke on this night. It hurt.

I noticed a ray of light through my balcony window. The sound of a strained, frozen engine grew louder, then stopped. I heard the faint slam of a car door and, knowing it was Scott, waited for my apartment buzzer to sound before getting up from the couch.

When I greeted him at the door, he exhaled, and we stood there watching each other. The thought of hugging him made me feel too vulnerable. So, I started "our fight" instead.

"Are you cheating on me?"

"I've had opportunities."

"Fuck you," flew out of my mouth. He followed my path back to the couch and we sat there angry, each waiting for the other to pull the next punch.

Scott hanging around with his friends at the bar on weekends didn't bother me until after I'd finished high school and our relationship grew more serious. That August, around my eighteenth birthday, he completely caught me off guard with a marriage proposal. I said yes, but no formal planning followed. There was no engagement ring or date set for the wedding. Maybe that's because we were both still out nightclubbing, living the singles scene, not really ready to give it up, not really admitting we weren't ready. Well, *I* wasn't admitting it. But one night, a month later, he did ...

> I snuggled in next to Scott on his mother's couch in front of an Oilers game on television. The popcorn bowl in front of us was empty, so he rose to refill it during a commercial break. When he returned and set it down in front of me, he paused, his hands extended toward me like a salesman ready to give his pitch.
>
> "What?" I smirked back at him. His mood had been a bit off all evening.
>
> "What if," he offered, "we take the next three months apart to, you know, go out with our friends ... get a few people out of our systems before we tie the knot for good?"
>
> I sat there baffled and speechless. Honesty is an important virtue in any partner, but this was taking it a little too far. My beautiful Scott turned ugly right before my eyes; my infatuation with him turned to indifference.
>
> "Well?" he asked. "What do you think?" As if he couldn't tell by the expression on my face.
>
> "Three months, eh?"
>
> "Yeah."

What was I going to say? "I guess that would be fine."

Truth be known, as far as I was concerned at that moment, he could take the rest of his life. It was one of those painful moments I carried around with me for many years to come, the one that always popped into my head whenever I knew he'd been out with "the boys."

Scott was first to break the silence. He reached into his pocket and pulled a crumpled bunch of pages out. "I never know what to say to you anymore," he sighed, handing them to me.

I took them and began to read aloud, "... *Katie, I can't sleep so I think I'll write instead. I have to admit I've been in a bit of a funk for the last year or so because no matter what I do, it's never right anymore. If my memory serves me correctly, you're the one who balked at moving in together the last time around. And I don't understand the problem with spending time with my friends at the bar, either. That's just what we do. I'm lucky to have as many good friends as I have. They do things with me that you can't or won't do anymore. Like ball games. Even if it's a bit cold out, they'll tough it out with me until the end ...* " I glared at him then, the angry tears brimming my eyes. "I'm *so* sorry if I don't stay out as late as I used to. I can't sleep in until noon like you do anymore. I have a child to get up with."

"See, you're overreacting *again*." He shook his head. "You *never* give me a chance."

"Fine." I continued my read. *"These are the 'nineties.' You don't have to be tied down or follow the same rules and guidelines our parents and grandparents did. For one thing, we live longer and have more opportunities now. Not to mention the fact that women have men by the balls nowadays. I know guys, especially, are not so eager to get married anymore. It's a huge financial risk, because we lose half if not more of everything we have if things don't work out. And the divorce rate is fifty percent ... "* Insulted, I threw the letter down and stormed from the room in frustration.

"Well, it's true," he called after me, halting me dead in my tracks.

I turned back to face him, my face flushed. "When have I *ever* asked you or any man to pay me child support? If I didn't go after Jason for what was rightfully mine back then, *why* would I go after something that's not mine now?" This was always the part that boiled my blood. He had known me for years. He knew I'd let Calvin's biological father go free. And if Scott was *that* afraid of a commitment, then why did he even bother showing up at my hospital room the day my son was born, wanting to try again? "You think *women* have men by the balls nowadays?" I grilled him. "Do you know what it's like to be a single parent? Sure, you get to be 'Mr. Nice-Guy,' taking Calvin out once a week for fun and treats. But *who* pays his day-care expenses and feeds him? *Who* takes him for hair cuts and helps him with his homework? *Who* has to discipline him while you get to be his best friend?"

Scott threw his arms up in resignation, and took his letter from the floor, storming down the hallway to collect his shoes. "You *always* do this. I never said I wouldn't help you out once in awhile."

"I've *never* demanded anything of you or tried to take anything from you." I protested. "And I resent the implication that I would."

"I'm talking about women in general."

"You can't generalize like that, Scott. Saying that *all* women are gold diggers is like me saying that *all* men are irresponsible fathers. It's not fair in either case, is it?"

Scott threw down his runners and braced himself to argue more. We stood there facing each other for what seemed like forever, two cats ready to pounce at the slightest hint of vulnerability. Our silence was finally broken by Scott taking my hand in his, and placing the crumpled letter from his fist back into my palm. "This isn't done yet." His eyes urged me to read on.

I exhaled and rubbed my forehead with my right hand, holding the pages out in front of me with my left. *"But I do love you, Katie. And you have to know how much I love Calvin. I love him like he's my own ... "* My voice broke then and I looked up at Scott. I couldn't argue that ...

"Can I hold him?" he asked, reaching his arms out a bit awkwardly, readying himself by leaning forward in his chair.

I handed my newborn to Scott and knelt down in front of them. "Make sure you support his head." I offered a pillow to help prop his arm.

Scott couldn't help chuckling at all of the faces Calvin made, such as scrunching up his little nose, pursing his lips together, and sticking out his tongue. We both sat there together, adoring every part of him: his perfectly manicured fingernails, his tiny little toes, his soft, rosy cheeks. It was so nice to be able to share this with someone, to know that he found it all as fascinating as I did.

And then Scott's eyes welled with tears. "Maybe this is the way it was supposed to be."

"What do you mean?" I asked.

He spoke softly as he stroked Calvin's tiny fingertips. "When I found out that my father had adopted me, I couldn't see how he could have loved me like he loved my younger brother and sister. They were his blood. I wasn't."

I squeezed his shoulder in support.

"I think this happened for a reason — you having this child that wasn't mine," he mused, "because if I can feel this way about *him*, I know my dad must have loved me, too."

"And maybe there's another reason it happened."

"What's that?"

"Some day Calvin is going to realize his own biological father isn't around. He's going to feel all sorts of things that you can relate to better than me. And you'll be able to help him through it."

Scott placed his palm on my cheek, rubbing away my tears with his thumb. "Do you want me to read the rest?" he offered.

I nodded yes, unable to speak at that moment. I knew where this was going.

We resumed our seats on the couch and he took the letter from me. "*When you drove to Calgary for that job interview last month, my heart broke. I know it hasn't been good for you financially in Saskatoon, and I want you to succeed, and I know you're going to do what you have to do. But I wonder what will become of us, of my relationship with Calvin ...* "

"Why can't you come with us?" I interrupted.

Scott set the letter down. "I'm happy *here*, Katlyn. My whole life is here: my job, my friends, my hockey."

I resented his job, his friends, his hockey. They seemed to make him happier than I did these days. And I resented that he was happy with his life, period, because I wasn't happy with mine. Maybe that was the greatest barrier between us. Maybe none of this had anything to do with the bar scene or tardiness ... or any of the other surface issues we argued about lately. Maybe this was simply about two people who had known each other since their teenage years, spending the better part of their lives together. And now, we were growing apart, finally recognizing our incompatibilities. I knew I was losing one of my best friends, my security blanket who had been with me through some of the toughest times in my life ...

Scott could tell I was tense, so he rubbed the back of my shoulder. My eyes were glued to the television. If I looked at him, I knew I would cry, and I didn't want to.

Then the phone rang. I looked at the clock on the wall. It was five minutes to eight. I rose to my feet to answer it. "Hello?"

"Come on," I heard Scott usher Calvin out of the room, into his bedroom.

My brother's voice sounded on the other end of the line, "He's gone."

"When?"

"About ten minutes ago. We just spent some time with him before I called you."

Out of the corner of my eye, I noticed Scott cautiously enter the room by himself. My hand involuntarily moved up to cover my face, my tears. The only word I could force out then was, "Okay," before hanging up the phone. I stood there for a bit, letting it all sink in. Then I turned to Scott and nodded. "Dad died."

Of course, he already knew that without my saying anything. He advanced toward me and hugged me close for as long as I needed. "I'm so sorry," he said. "It'll be okay."

Once I'd regained my composure, I looked up at him and smiled. "I *am* okay." He smiled back at me. I asked him to leave, so I could be alone with my thoughts, and he didn't question me for a minute. He put on his coat and gave me one last kiss before leaving my apartment, gently closing the door behind him. He did everything right. He knew me like no one else.

This was also about Calvin. Scott had been there for him since day one when his own father had chosen not to be. Sure, he never lived with us, never married me, or legally adopted Calvin. But his heart was with that kid and always would be. I knew that much.

Scott and I had known each other long enough at this point that we didn't have to say we were sorry to know the argument was over. We just instinctively knew it was, and we moved in a bit closer to one another. He placed his arm around me, a sombre expression on his face. "People keep telling me it's only a matter of time before Calvin and I grow apart. He's going to forget me when you move."

"People keep telling me the same thing," I admitted.

"I don't want that to happen, Katie."

"Then we won't let it happen," I said. "What other people think is irrelevant."

* * *

Calvin and I moved a month later. To the bitter end, there were more disagreements between us as we adjusted to my decision. This wasn't going to be like the other times we had broken up, where it was only a matter of time before we reconciled again. This was permanent. We were now in separate provinces.

Scott and I both moved on with our lives and eventually began dating other people. There were the inevitable emotions and hard feelings over the years as we figured out our new place in each other's lives. But through it all, Scott remained true to his devotion to Calvin. His regular phone calls and visits continued on as promised, even when my own visits back home became fewer and farther between. His love for "his son" never wavered.

As the years passed and other relationships came and went, I was more and more grateful for this one constant in Calvin's life.

Time Flies

I guess what brought it on was my own disappointment with life in general. What had I made of myself? I was twenty-seven years old, and still hadn't accomplished anything out of the ordinary. My adolescent dream of becoming the next Barbara Frum (of course, a more stunningly attractive version of her) was nothing more than ... well, just that: an adolescent dream. Nothing was turning out how I'd always imagined it to. I wasn't supposed to be an inside sales representative for a newspaper, scraping by every month, living in a cramped two-bedroom apartment, dating "the wrong guy" after "the wrong guy." I was supposed to be a happily married, successful journalist by now, with my gorgeous, corporate husband, and our healthy, happy son and daughter — all living together blissfully on our vast acreage on the outskirts of town.

The more I dwelled on present circumstances, the more I found myself pulling out old high-school love letters from my closet, trying to relive my glory days when I was someone special — not just another social insurance number the government mails child tax credits to every month. I started thinking about my first love, Brent. He'd moved away with his parents to Grimsby, Ontario, right after graduating high school. I'd thought about him through the years from time to time, but it became more of an obsession when I was feeling down. It seemed every other night, I was poring over my old photo albums or reading his notes and cards as though he'd written them to me yesterday. I resurrected all of the old tapes he'd made me in high school, listening to our favourite hits from the eighties. One evening, I went so far as to drive down to our old make-out spot by the river, parking there for awhile, all in an attempt to recapture our time together. I couldn't get him out of my head. Even after the move to Calgary.

Maybe it wasn't so much him I was missing, but that time in my life when everything was right — the age of innocence before all the crap, the last time I remember feeling strong and secure. I was turning fifteen. My family was all together. I had a flourishing social life, a boyfriend who adored me, and not a care in the world other than final exams and attending weekend parties. Hard to believe more than twelve years had already passed. It all went by so quickly, faster than I'd ever imagined.

One night, I had this bizarre dream that I was aimlessly wandering the residential streets of Grimsby, trying to find Brent's home. For whatever reason, I ended up parking my car six blocks away from his house, hiking through mud puddles, over fences, around yards, in 4-inch heels and a torn cocktail dress. When I found my way there, his parents (who looked nothing like his parents in the dream) greeted me at the door, and I sat with them at their kitchen table, awaiting his arrival. Brent appeared around the corner, standing in the hallway, wearing a dishevelled blue robe and fuzzy, green slippers. Without even a word, he approached my side of the table, kissing me so passionately that it felt real. That's what woke me up. I couldn't concentrate on anything else all day. I kept rerunning that scene inside my mind, not wanting to lose the flood of desire it filled me with. It had been such a long time since I'd felt anything that intense, so I suppose that's what finally triggered my quest to find him again, to talk to him again. The photo albums were no longer enough.

For several weeks, I battled with myself over phoning him. More than twelve years had passed since the last time we spoke; who knew if he was still in Grimsby. And what if he was? What if I found him? What if he was involved with someone else? God, I'd feel like such a fool! Here I was, still unattached, a single parent working unfulfilling jobs, with no more focus in life than when I graduated from high school. How could I face him? That's not what you want people to know. You want to be able to run into someone from your past and say, "Yeah, things are great! I married a wealthy banker a few years back. We have two wonderful children and a beautiful home. I've just finished my journalism degree and was hired by a local television station as their prime-time news anchor ... " I don't know, something like that. You just want to make it sound good, and no matter how good it actually is, you want to make it sound better.

But then there was the other side of the coin: what if he was still single, too? What if he'd been wondering as much about me as I was about him and neither of us made the first move? Talk about a missed opportunity. Then again, did I really want him back? Would we even be compatible after all these years? A lot of things had changed in my life. Probably in his, too. We weren't kids anymore.

I stared at my phone night after night, trying to gather enough courage to take that first step. A couple of times, I picked up the receiver and listened to the dial tone, but I could never bring myself to push the buttons. I still had his parents' phone number in my Rolodex after all those years. I took the card out one night and stared at it, debating making the call. Then it dawned on me that he was thirty years old by now — he probably had a place of his own — so, I picked up the phone and dialed information to see if he was listed.

"Directory assistance for what city please?"

"Grimsby." I balanced a notebook on my trembling knees and held my pen steady to jot his number down.

"For what name?"

"Brent Johnson."

I could hear her typing on the keyboard. "I don't have a Brent or B. Johnson listed, ma'am."

"Damn it," I scolded under my breath. "Thanks anyway," I said, hanging up the phone.

I pulled his parents' card from my Rolodex, holding it firmly with my left hand, flicking it with my fingertip. How was I going to get around this? Calling Brent was agonizing enough, let alone having to encounter his parents in the process. The mere thought of it reduced me to the awkward teenager who sat lost for words at their dining-room table on the two or three occasions I'd had dinner with them.

Okay. This is ridiculous! You're an adult now! You can do this! Just in case I decided to bail at the last minute, I dialed *67 before their telephone number, so they wouldn't be able to trace the call. Yeah, you're an adult, all right.

I dialed their number, my heart pounding so hard that I could feel the veins in my neck pulsating. I waited four long rings before someone finally picked up. "Hello?" a deep voice answered. Shit. It's his dad of all people.

I cleared my throat. "Um, yes, hello. I'm wondering if you can tell me how I might be able to reach Brent."

"Well, that depends on who this is," he answered slyly.

Oh God. My face burned red as I switched the receiver from one sweaty palm to the other. "Katie." I answered reluctantly, assuming that he would know who "Katie" was after all these years.

Adding even more embarrassment to the situation, he didn't remember me at all. "Katie who?"

Oh Jesus. I exhaled. "Katlyn Wright. From Saskatoon." There went my cover.

I could hear him thinking out loud. "Katlyn ... Katlyn ... " It may have been genuine hesitation, but the cynic in me told me it was more for his own amusement. He'd always been a bit of a tease with me, given how easily I blushed. "Oh, *Katie*!" he finally said, "How *are* you?"

"Fine. How are you?" I answered with forced cheeriness, just wanting this to be over.

"Well, I'm fine, but you know, Brent is married now. He's expecting his first child in three months."

My worst nightmare had come true. It was too late to hang up, because he already knew who I was. So, I tried being witty with, "Oh well, I guess his wife wouldn't appreciate me phoning then, would she?" followed by a pathetic, uncomfortable chuckle.

"Probably not. But give me your number and I'll pass it on to him."

For the love of God! Give him my number? I was not prepared to answer any more questions, so I recited the first ten digits that popped into my head — my old area code and number in Saskatoon — and tried bringing our conversation to a close before I dug myself in any deeper. "Well, it's been really nice talking to you again," I lied.

"You, too," he answered. But he didn't leave it at that. "So, how've you been? Are you married yet?"

Like I'd be calling if I was? This was getting worse by the minute. "Uh, yes. Well, no. Well, engaged. I'm engaged. We're both trying to get our careers on track before we get married."

"I see," he said. I was pretty sure he knew I was full of shit. I was certain he was enjoying every minute of it, too. "So, where do you work? Are you still in school?"

As a teenager, I'd always boasted to everyone that I was going to be a journalist, so the next thing I knew, I was, "a freelance reporter for the StarPhoenix," keeping it consistent with the fact that I'd told him I was still in Saskatoon.

"Well, good for you!" he cheered. "And what does your fiancé, do?"

Good question. Let's hope the next one isn't 'What's his name?' "He's a branch manager with the Royal Bank," I bragged. What was I doing? I was making it worse with each sentence I spoke!

"Well, it's been so good to hear from you," he said. At last, I was off the hook. Or, was I? "Listen, Brent's mom is here. I'm sure she'd love to talk to you. Hold on a minute." He abandoned the phone.

Before I had the opportunity to object, he was off the line. All I could hear was his distant voice and the clatter of pots and pans in the background. Heaven knows this isn't already humiliating enough. Why don't I talk to the whole damn family?

I sat there, waiting, and waiting, cupping a hand over my strained eyes, my head nodding back and forth from the sheer embarrassment of it all. "Katie?" her voice sounded after the muffled receiver was released into her hands.

"Hi, Mrs. Johnson. How are you?"

"I'm fine! How are you? Are you married yet?"

"Engaged." I sank further into my chair.

"So, what are you doing now?"

My head fell back and I privately cursed the ceiling above. "I work for the StarPhoenix in Saskatoon."

"Good for you!"

Okay, that was enough. No more questions about me. The next thing I knew, I'd be a millionaire living in some river-front mansion. "What about you? How are things over there?"

"Well, Brent's father and I are elated! We're expecting our first grandchild in the fall. Brent and his wife live in Toronto, now. He's a guard at the penitentiary there."

At least *someone* had fulfilled his childhood dream. Brent had always talked about becoming a police officer some day. He'd also always wanted to marry and have a big family. Now, he was on his way to that, too. "How is everyone else?" I asked, trying to change the subject to something a bit more tolerable.

"We're all fine. Derrick is managing a pet store in Alberta and David just graduated from high school."

My eyes popped open. "*David* just graduated from high school? That kid was in Kindergarten the last time I saw him!"

"Hard to believe," she agreed. "Where does the time go?"

We talked for a while longer. I agreed to visit them if I was ever in the area — as if! — and we wished each other all the best. When I hung up the phone, I pulled my photo album out, flipping through its pages one last time. I feel like such a jerk. I feel like such a fool. A tear streamed down my face.

Before that night, and that conversation, Brent and I still existed in my mind as all those years ago. Everything seemed as it appeared in my faded photographs, offering solace whenever I needed. A part of me wished I hadn't made the call, because now the one "escape" I had was no longer available to me. But I had to do it; I had to know, or I may have been wondering indefinitely.

As I turned each page, it wasn't so much the pictures of Brent that affected me, but the ones of his younger brother, David. It was hard to picture that mischievous, little boy with his blue, Slurpie-stained tongue sticking out at the camera now wearing a cap and gown, and clutching a high-school diploma in his hand. He was nearly thirteen years older now. So was I. It was time to move forward instead of clinging to the past.

Still, wouldn't it be perfect if old flames always carried a torch for you even if you didn't love them anymore? Wouldn't it be nice if they never moved on with their lives as you moved on with yours?

Gay

"*How* about a top-up?" I tipped the wine bottle over Cameron's glass and poured.

"Thank you."

Dry, white wine was definitely one thing we had in common. Since we'd begun dating six months earlier, seldom an evening spent together passed without polishing off a small bottle. I think it helped us relax through the awkward lulls that sometimes burdened our conversations.

With Cameron nearly twelve years my senior, I anticipated a few obstacles along the way ... different tastes in music, pastimes ... trivial details like these. Getting to know him was a slow process, but there were enough positives to keep me interested. Like the way we kissed, touched. The way he pulled his chair around to my side of the table at restaurants, nestling in close to share my menu while his own lay closed. He could be very affectionate when he wanted to be.

We'd discussed marriage, hypothetically, on one or two occasions to get a feel for one another's life philosophies. Already into his forties, Cameron was hedging a bit on starting a family of his own, but hadn't ruled it out altogether. His only concern was with day-care. He expressed a preference for a more traditional family lifestyle, in which his wife would stay home with the children and he would be the sole provider. This was quite a bit different from my vision of the future — one that didn't involve more diapers. I was career-minded, finally earning a decent living in advertising sales. After eight struggling years of parenting alone, I felt I was halfway to the finish line. I was not at all interested in going back to the starting line. These next few years were mine to branch out and explore, begin saving for Calvin's education and my retirement, now that I'd finally wiped out my debt. I saw these differences between us as a mere wrinkle that would need ironing down the road, but did not foresee any other relationship-breaking issues. Until this evening ...

"Oh, Grant phoned the other night," Cameron interrupted my psychoanalyzing. "He's passing through Calgary on Wednesday, on his way to his aunt's." Grant was a friend of Cameron's dating back to their early twenties when they'd both lived up near Edmonton. They'd been with the same employer for ten years, sharing a house as roommates for the last five. Then, Grant moved west to British Columbia and Cameron transferred to Calgary with his construction company.

I settled on the futon beside Cameron. One day, I wouldn't be entertaining my guests on a futon; someday soon, I'd buy a new couch. "Is he crashing overnight?"

"That's the plan."

I followed his eyes to the television screen, where a lawyer and his buxom defendant savoured a steamy embrace. I snuggled in a bit closer. "Looks like *they've* got the right idea."

Cameron smiled.

I recalled the first time I'd seen that smile, at a friend's garden wedding in the summer. I'd been coached ahead of time to watch for the rugged blonde. He was available and, if I was interested, the girls would put in a good word for me. After all, how enjoyable is a life with a thriving career and no one to share it all with, they asked. True enough.

Back then, I found Cameron's reticence mysterious, even intriguing. But lately, it was taking on a whole different meaning. If we couldn't communicate, what did we have? Great chemistry can only take you so far. I decided that my futon would remain in its upright position tonight until we each bared our hearts and minds.

"What about Grant?" was the first topic to enter my mind. I propped myself back up beside him. "How come I never see him with anyone?"

"Busy with work, I guess."

"Well, are there any prospects, or is he just not interested?"

Cameron smirked. "No. He's *gay*." He shook his head with a quiet chuckle.

"Well, it wouldn't bother me if he was," I replied matter-of-factly. "Someone very close to me is gay."

Cameron's posture stiffened. "Who?"

"Alex."

"Your *brother*?" His eyes widened.

"Is that a problem?"

His discomfort was pronounced by a mouthful of air he held in, rolling it back and forth between his cheeks before releasing it slowly, emphatically. He didn't look at me. He *couldn't* look at me. A problem? It obviously was.

I watched him, my eyes moistening. "Cam, come on," I coaxed, gently reaching for his arm.

He recoiled, and threw his hands up in one involuntary motion. "I'm sorry. It just makes me really uncomfortable."

Of all the topics I could have chosen, why did we end up with *this* one? "Well, I'm glad we got this out into the open when we did," I fibbed, trying hard to appear unaffected. Of course, anyone who knew me well enough knew incessant chatter was a sure sign of nerves. A two-minute spiel on my loyalty to Alex followed; he would always be welcome in my home — with or without his dates — and my future husband, whomever it may be, would just have to learn to accept that.

Overkill. Cameron stared back in terror.

"Well, aren't you going to say anything?" I persisted. "Is this going to create that much of a problem between us?"

A few times, it looked as though Cameron might speak, but each time his mouth opened, it closed; each time he lifted his hands, they fell. Until finally, "I don't know," came out from under his breath. He rinsed his mouth with a sip of wine and swallowed hard.

The truth was, this had been a tacit fear of mine ever since the day my brother courageously revealed his homosexuality to our family. I loved him — knowing this didn't change my feelings for him — but I had to admit, the issue was foreign to me. I didn't understand it because it was uncommon where I'd grown up. And I feared the day may come when I would be judged by association by a homophobic friend. Now here I was, and it was happening. I'd never felt so rejected in all my life.

This must have been how Alex felt whenever he heard gay jokes followed by laughter. At a time when homosexuality was still very hush-hush, he'd gone through his teen years feeling isolated and ashamed, feeling as though there was no one to talk to who would understand, let alone relate. He once told me that he'd struggled with his sexuality since pre-pubescence. He'd suppressed the emotions for years, dating as many girls as he could, hoping it would somehow influence his nature. But, of course, it didn't. His journey to self-acceptance was an arduous one that lasted well into adulthood.

I looked at Cameron who was now across the room, solemnly staring through the window, into the darkness. "I can't believe this." I rubbed my temples. "Is this *really* all that bad?"

"Well, if you're asking me whether or not we'll break up over this, I can't answer you tonight."

My jaw hung open, all kinds of profanities itching the tip of my tongue. Alex may be patient with people's disrespect, but I certainly wasn't going to tolerate Cameron's. Wet mascara stinging my eyes, I advanced toward the door, and flung it open, standing at its side. "Get out." My voice was calm although my heart was pounding. I didn't know what else to do at that moment.

"Get out?" Cameron repeated.

"You heard me."

He was glaring at me now. "I told you that I'm uncomfortable with this and that's not going to change overnight. But you're telling me that if I can't come to terms with it right this minute, we're over?"

"No, *you're* the one who's saying there's a possibility we may break up over this," I argued. "So what other choice do I have? How can I let myself fall in love with you when, at any time, you might drop the bomb and tell me we're through because you can't deal with it?"

Cameron fell back against the wall, his arms crossed in front, his eyes cursing the ceiling above. "What do you want from me? I mean, what did you expect, Katlyn? Honestly."

"Well, I certainly didn't expect *this*." My eyes shifted to my son Calvin's bedroom door where I heard rustling. I closed the main door and walked toward his room. It provided the perfect escape from what must have been the most uncomfortable moment I'd ever lived.

My son was fast asleep as I knelt down beside him, pulling the comforter back over his shoulders to keep him warm. I stayed there with him for a time. If only Cameron knew Alex the way we knew him: what an accomplished musician and language teacher he was, the way Calvin's eyes lit up whenever his uncle came to visit. I didn't realize until this night how much I resented the unfounded stereotypes certain people held toward homosexuals, presuming that they're all promiscuous freaks with no regard for convention. Alex, who was in a monogamous relationship, was a true gentleman and deserved people's respect. I wanted my Calvin to grow up knowing that, recognizing that. I didn't want him to have the same fear and bias as previous generations.

When I went back out to the other room, Cameron returned to the futon on cue, retrieving the remote control from under the piled cushions. "There's got to be *something* on," he fussed, surfing the channels, his feet perched back up on the coffee table like nothing had happened.

"No," I lunged toward him, taking the remote from his hands, and turning the television off. I placed the remote on a bookshelf across the room, out of arm's reach. "No. This is not going to disappear, Cam. You can't just ignore it now."

"Okay."

"Look ... " I took my seat beside him, searching for the right words, *any* words. "I know — I know this is hard for some people. It took my family some getting used to, as well."

"Well, if you can understand that they needed time to accept it, why all the pressure on me?"

"I thought I was losing you. Am I?"

Cameron's silence broke my heart again.

"Do you think it's a choice?" I asked at last. "Because it's not. Some people are left-handed while most are right. Homosexuality is in some people's genes just as heterosexuality is in ours."

Cameron wiped the palms of his hands down the front of his jeans. "If that's the case ... " he considered my analogy for a moment, "then does that mean *you* could have gay children? That it's in your genes? He *is* your brother."

I wasn't sure if I should laugh or cry — that he would reconsider our relationship based solely on the possibility that I might have gay children bordered on the offensive. "*You* might very well produce gay children," I staidly informed. "You're not anymore 'immune' to this than *I* am. Than anyone, for that matter." And why did we have to talk about this like it was a disease, anyway? Just because something is a minority doesn't mean it's an abnormality.

"I highly doubt that," he replied. "No one in my family is gay."

"No one that you know of. Maybe they've never felt they could 'come out' with all the gay jokes your family throws around."

My suggestion did not sit well with Cameron. He returned to his taciturn self for the remainder of the evening. He was right about one thing, I decided — we weren't going to resolve this in one night.

I rose, collected the wine glasses, tossing the remote control back into his hands on my way to the kitchen. What a night. What a crazy conversation. I rinsed the glasses under the hot tap, setting them to dry on a tea towel on the counter.

Now, suddenly, it was *me* questioning the future of our relationship. Did I want to spend my life hiding this secret from Cameron's family members? Should I live my life feeling quietly ashamed, as though I was somehow betraying my brother whenever I played along and giggled at one of their remarks about gays? And did I want to feel uncomfortable in my own home, or have Alex and his friends feel unwelcome around my family whenever they came to visit? Or maybe Alex would stop visiting altogether. I also considered Calvin. He was still young enough to be influenced in his views about homosexuals. Did I want him growing up with the same misguided notions Cameron held, in turn causing confusion about his feelings for his own uncle?

"The Simpsons are on!" Cameron's voice startled me from the other room.

I dabbed a tissue below my eyes. "Yeah, coming."

Cameron lay lengthwise on the futon with enough room for me to squeeze in front. He patted the space in front of him, an invitation to join him. It felt good to cradle into his warmth, to feel his arm across my waist. The silence between us had never been more comforting.

Never My Family

As a child growing up in small-town Saskatchewan, I really took my freedom for granted. On weekends or summer holidays, I would wake up at eight o'clock in the morning, dress, eat my cereal, and dart out the back door to play with friends. I'd say all of four words — "Bye mom! Bye dad!" — before disappearing from their sight until the hunger pangs in my stomach told me it was time to go home for lunch. I had my own social life. I was free to be myself and to act my age without prying adult eyes watching my every move, cramping my style. My parents didn't have to worry about me; they knew where I was. They knew all of the parents and kids on our block. Everyone knew everyone, and abuse was something that happened somewhere else. Not in Lanigan. Not in any of our families. We were safe.

My son has never known true freedom — not in the way I have. Maybe a big part of the difference was due to living in cities rather than a small town. There seemed to be a different mentality in the city, particularly one as large as Calgary. People weren't as trusting and everyone seemed chronically rushed. I didn't even know most of my neighbours by name. Once in awhile, they'd be running in while I was flying out, and we'd acknowledge each other with a smile, but that was the extent of our relationship. I knew nothing about them, really. And I never took the time to learn more. I'm not sure why.

I don't know. Maybe it wasn't the city at all. Maybe it was simply the times we were now living in. Co-workers of mine spoke about growing up in Calgary and how safe it had once been, as much as any small town. They recalled taking off down the street on their bikes every summer morning, just as I had, meeting friends at nearby parks to make-believe the day away. Here we

were, twenty years later, and I was uneasy about letting
my son play alone in the backyard. What had happened?
What had changed? Or, was I just being paranoid?

Not knowing many of our neighbours made it that
much more difficult to find friends on the block for
Calvin to play with. As a result, he had to learn how to
entertain himself, especially on the weekends I wasn't
chauffeuring him around to his school friends' houses.
Up until he was nine, the farthest I would let him ride
his bike was back and forth in front of our home, within
eyeshot in either direction. You can imagine how much
fun *that* was for him. Of course, the day came when that
range was no longer satisfying, and he asked if he could
ride around the block. "I'll be fine, mom," he assured
me, those shiny brown eyes of his melting mine.

I knew I had to give him his space. The more I
declined the little things, the more he would rebel later
on. All the way around the block, though? We lived on a
busy street in a city I was not yet familiar with. What if
he was hit by a car? What if there was a group of older
kids, waiting for a little boy like Calvin to ride by so they
could tease him and steal his bike? What if a stranger
pulled up beside him, sweet-talked him toward the car,
and then plucked him from the street, taking my baby
away from me forever? I don't know how long I stood
there thinking this through, my arms crossed, my foot
tapping nervously on the ground. "Okay," I said at last.
"You can go; however, there are a few rules ... "

"Yes!" Calvin rejoiced.

I followed him down the stairs, out the back door to
where his bike stood waiting. He put on his helmet and I
helped him fasten the straps. "You make sure this stays
on at all times, you hear me?"

"Yes," he beamed.

"And you stay on the sidewalk. If I catch you on the
road even once, that'll be the last time you ... "

"I know," he said, still smiling, hopping on his bike.

"And no talking to strangers! And watch for cars!" He was already halfway down the sidewalk with me shouting after him, "And no dilly-dallying on the other side!" And he was gone.

I went back into our duplex and stood by the window, nervously watching, waiting. I couldn't concentrate on anything else. It seemed like forever before Calvin reappeared around the block, on his way back up the street. Then, and only then, did I breathe.

Each day Calvin went biking around the block and returned home safely. Each day it got a little easier to let him go. And then one day, he showed up at the house with a little boy named Jordan. The two of them wanted to play in Calvin's room. Jordan seemed like a nice enough kid, and I was thrilled that my Calvin had found a new friend. Still, I didn't know this child's parents and that concerned me. "Let's go over to your house and meet your mom, first," I told Jordan. "I don't want her to worry about you."

As it turned out, Jordan lived at the end of our block. His mother peered through the kitchen window as we entered the yard. "Can I go over to my new friend's house?" her son called to her from the gate.

I smiled, patting him on the head. "Hi, I'm Katlyn. This is my son Calvin."

"Hi, I'm Cindy," she replied through the screen. I couldn't help noticing that she looked tired. Then again, I probably looked pretty tired myself some days. Kids will do that to you.

"Listen, we live down the block, on the corner. Is it okay with you if Jordan comes over for awhile?" I asked.

"I guess so," she said. "Just make sure he's home in half an hour for supper."

"No problem." It occurred to me that the boys might want to play again another day. It might be a good idea to exchange phone numbers, so I asked. Cindy left the window briefly and returned with a pen and paper, jotting down my number for herself. She passed hers through a tear in the screen. Cindy never did leave her house. I thought that was a bit strange, but I didn't dwell on it.

The boys played in Calvin's room for awhile. Shortly after, they marched past me in the kitchen, each equipped with a plastic sword and shield, on their way outside to the backyard. It made me smile; they looked so cute. "Don't take off without telling me!" I called after them.

I kept a close eye on the clock, not wanting Jordan to return home late from his first visit to our place. When his half hour was up, I went outside to let them know. But they weren't in the backyard.

A man lounged in a lawn chair next door. He saw my panicked expression and motioned with his hand, "They went around the front."

"Thanks!" I sighed with relief. Little buggers.

I got to the front just in time to see Calvin riding up the sidewalk. His face looked serious and he was panting as he spoke. "Jordan was trying out my bike! He was riding it really fast and he fell off and hurt himself!"

My heart almost jumped out my chest. "Where is he? Is he okay?"

"He ran home!" my son informed me.

I felt completely responsible, cursing myself for letting them out of my sight. Jordan's own bike was still in our yard, so I picked it up, dusted it off, and started walking it back to his house. Calvin took off ahead of me, returning shortly after, his face flushed. "What's wrong?" I asked him.

"Is Jordan's dad ever *mean*."

"What happened?" I was even more concerned now.

"He told me to get the hell out of here. He said we're done playing."

That didn't sound very good to me at all. I was cautious turning the corner, guiding Jordan's bike up the walk to his yard, not sure what to expect when I got there. That's when I saw a lanky man standing in the yard beside a smoking barbecue: unshaven, unkempt, two empty beer bottles in one hand, and a full bottle in the other.

I carefully opened the gate, propping Jordan's bike against the inside fence. "Jordan left this at our place. Is everything okay?"

The man took a swig of his drink and grumbled, "That fuckin' kid. He's always playing too rough. He's fuckin' grounded."

My eyes popped wide open.

Then, the back door to their house opened a crack. I could see a woman's hand on the inside doorknob and strands of stringy, blonde hair falling down the side of her arm. "Never mind," Cindy's husband scolded her. "Nothin' to see out here." The door pulled closed on his command.

Shaken by the scene, I instinctively grabbed my son by the arm and ushered him away from their yard. My God, if this was how Jordan's father reacted when his son fell off his bike, then … The thought sent shivers down my spine.

My heart sank when I looked down at Calvin: his first friend on the street and he'd already lost him. There was no way I'd ever let him go anywhere near that yard again. I placed my hand on his shoulder, gently bringing him to a standstill. I knelt down in front of him on the sidewalk. "Calvin," I hesitated. "I don't want you going over there anymore."

He shrugged his shoulders. "Why?"

I had to think about it for a minute. How do you explain these things to a kid? "Honey, I don't want you to be rude to Jordan or ignore him if you see him on the street, but you're not to set foot in his yard again. I don't like the way his dad talked to you. I don't like the way he talked to *anyone* over there. Do you understand?"

"He's pretty mean," he nodded.

I continued letting Calvin ride his bike around the block after that episode. I couldn't very well take his new-found freedom away, now could I? That would seem like a punishment for doing nothing wrong. Still, it was hard to let him go. Sure, *this* time he was lucky. *This* time, I got involved soon enough to intervene. What about the next time? What about in a year or two, when the confines of our block would no longer suffice and he'd want those boundaries increased again?

Calvin wasn't the only person I was concerned about. I often thought of Jordan and his mom, even though I never did dial their phone number to let them know that. I threw the number away instead. My first instinct was avoidance. I didn't want to get involved with "that kind of family," or have my son influenced by them in any way. As much as one part of me worried about Cindy, another side of me wondered what was keeping her there. I mean, she could leave if she really wanted to. Couldn't she? So, what on earth made her stay? What was it that attracted her to a man like that in the first place? I figured if she had a good head on her shoulders, she would have seen the signs of what was to come. She would never have married him in the first place, let alone have a child with him.

I couldn't understand the mentality and, to be perfectly honest, felt I was somehow above it. Nor did I consider it my problem. People like that — you can't help them, I told myself. Thank God my mother had raised me with enough good sense to avoid such catastrophes. I would never find myself in an abusive situation like that. I was immune.

Or so I believed at the time ...

Whirlwind

----- Original Message -----
From: Katlyn
To: An Internet Help Line
Sent: Monday, August 19, 8:33 PM
Subject: Help

I was surfing the Internet tonight when I came across your website and thought you might be able to help. I have never felt so disoriented. Reading your page has been both validating and disturbing at the same time. It seems to match my circumstances very closely and yet maybe I'm wrong. I don't know anything for sure anymore.

Last summer, I started dating a man I'll call "Bryan," whom I'd known through friends at work for a couple of years. Everyone had such wonderful things to say about him; I decided to take the chance, and we very quickly fell in love. It's never happened for me like that before. Until Bryan, I'd never felt like any man was my soul mate. There's that saying: you'll know he's "the one" because he'll be different from all the rest. Well, this one was definitely different.

It was a whirlwind romance. It all happened so quickly; I'm ashamed to admit it now. But I really thought I knew him, you know? It's not as though we were a couple of twenty-year-olds lacking life experience: I'd just turned thirty and he was five years older than that; we both had stable, well-paying careers with the same company; we'd both been raising children on our own for years. The thing that struck me was how easily it all seemed to unfold between us. It was effortless. After several evenings talking the hours away, I learned that all of his life philosophies matched mine to a tee. He was so positive, complimentary, charismatic, and understanding. And he wasn't at all afraid of a commitment like so many of the others before him. He accepted me completely, flaws and all. In fact, the sooner we were married, all the better in his mind. We were engaged within four weeks and set our wedding date for December.

I didn't own a home yet, but Bryan owned a farm east of the city and would commute the hour into work each day. Even though I'd never lived in the country and knew nothing about that lifestyle, he had this way of making me fall in love with the whole idea of it. We eventually agreed that rather than buying a new place together, my son and I would move out there with him and his adolescent daughter after the wedding. It just made the most sense at the time.

About four or five weeks before the wedding date, my instinct started telling me to postpone the wedding. I can't pinpoint why, exactly. I just had this increasing uneasiness about the whole thing. Bryan seemed to be growing a bit more jealous, showing up unexpectedly at my place in the evenings, as though to make sure I was home alone. A few times he showed up despite having a shift scheduled at work. He was also extremely upset when I wanted to attend my grandmother's funeral out of town, saying that he was afraid something would happen and I wouldn't come back. So, little things like that. I had also noticed that Bryan could drink quite a bit — a lot more than I was accustomed to, anyway.

One night, I finally gathered the courage to tell him I wanted to postpone the wedding until the summer, because it all seemed to be happening too fast for me. I said this didn't mean it was over between us; I still loved him and wanted to stay together. But he was devastated nonetheless. He told me that I was ruining his life. Angrily, he hurled his beer bottle across the room, smashing it against the wall beside me. Of course,

I felt terrible. He must love me so deeply to feel such strong emotions. How could I do this to him?

We talked about it all at length in the days that followed. Bryan called and visited more often than before. He insisted that I didn't have to be frightened of the future and everything was going to be fine. Marriage was not going to change a thing. I could still have my career, hobbies, and individuality; I would just be sharing them with him, that's all. He said I was simply afraid of the unknown, experiencing the natural hesitation we all do before the big day. Everyone gets a little crazy during these emotionally charged times, he reasoned, and the beer bottle incident was his moment — just like the "cold feet" were mine. It was an isolated incident, he assured me — simply his reaction after a stressful day. Several times he hugged me and said there was no reason to overreact.

After much deliberation, I decided he was probably right; my fears probably *were* irrational. After all of the money and emotion we'd already invested in this, I'd be crazy to walk away. Both our children seemed really excited for the wedding and the prospect of becoming a "real" family. We'd already told so many people. I felt such pressure from it all, you know? I didn't want to disappoint anyone or look like a fool. So, I married him in December as planned. And when I walked up to that altar five months after our first date, I entered into marriage determined to make it work. I believed I truly loved him, and I believed he truly loved me. I went into this deciding we were going to prove all the skeptics wrong — that it *is* possible to have a lasting marriage even though it all happened so quickly.

Our first month of marriage was blissful. Bryan was so caring, so affectionate. When he returned home from his night shifts, he would warm my car for me each morning, make fresh coffee, pouring me a cup for the road. When I got to work, there would be love songs waiting for me on my voice mail or flowers delivered in the afternoon. I thought I must be the luckiest woman in the world.

Then one day I got a phone call from him at work. He was crying, clearly devastated after finding an old photo album of mine. There were pictures of an old boyfriend inside, and Bryan felt it was disrespectful that I still held onto them. I thought it strange that he was *this* emotional over such a minor detail, especially since there were still wedding photos of his first marriage displayed both in his daughter's room and our basement. I had accepted their right to these memories without question. So, how was my having pictures tucked away on a shelf any different? But it obviously was different from his perspective. He wanted the photos gone. I assured him that I would remove them later that week.

I didn't intend to get rid of them altogether. I was just going to put them away somewhere out of sight, out of mind. Two nights later, after Bryan had gone to work and the children were in bed, I went to retrieve the album only to find a letter he'd taped to the cover. In his note, he sincerely apologized, writing that he just had to do it because he'd been so upset he'd puked. Do *what*? I felt sick as I opened the album. Pages and pages of photographs were missing! Dozens of them. Even some that didn't include the old boyfriend in them. When Bryan returned home from work late that night, he sheepishly admitted he'd thrown them all in the burning barrel outside and destroyed them. He begged for my forgiveness in tears.

I felt so violated. Honestly, it was tantamount to rape. This was *my* personal property; it was therefore *my* right to decide whether or not I should keep it. Yet, at the same time, he wasn't just a boyfriend anymore — he was my husband — so I tried not to "overreact." They're just photographs, I told myself. And Bryan seemed genuinely remorseful about the whole thing. He said he just loved me so much that he'd lost his head for a moment, but it would never happen again. He promised.

Our marriage went downhill very quickly from there. It was as though Bryan tightened his grip more with each passing day. All of a sudden, I could do nothing right in this man's eyes. He was unusually suspicious of my every move, accusing me of not being devoted to him and the kids if I didn't spend every waking moment outside of work with them. My once positive Bryan who'd shared all my life philosophies now seemed to find the negative in everything I did: my fitness regime was "stupid;" my wanting to take professional golf lessons with friends from work rather than from him alone was "offensive;" and, I should no longer belong to speaking groups such as Toastmasters because "day-long social situations are no place for married women." Not to mention the day I came home from work to find he'd opened my personal mail before I'd had the chance.

I tried to be diplomatic and honest with him about these things, hoping we could come to some sort of a compromise. But we never seemed to have a meaningful conversation about anything. Instead, Bryan felt attacked and accused me of not loving him, of not wanting to be married. During what should have been minor disagreements between a husband and a wife, I would watch him fly into rages, spouting hurtful accusations that left my head spinning. Only a month and a half into our marriage, the same man who had been so angry with me for wanting to postpone the wedding *now* proclaimed he had married me "under false pretences" and the marriage was a huge mistake. "Someday we'll have a discussion about how marriage *really* is!" he told me. Of course, he refused to follow through with that discussion. Instead, he stormed out of the house, slamming the door behind him, leaving me to sit there stewing in my own juices, while trying to absorb what had just happened.

The tension rose. The more I tried to reason with him, the more desperate the measures he took to try to manipulate me. He started using the children as pawns, saying that I obviously didn't love them and he knew my son was "a mistake." He said they'd both told him they felt neglected when I spent time writing speeches for Toastmasters in the evening. Although, he could never tell me what was actually said. When I asked, he would change the subject.

I tried. I really tried to rearrange my schedule so that no one would feel unloved or left out. But nothing was ever good enough. When I planned to take the family to a park for the day, all Bryan could do was complain in front of the kids about what a lame idea it was to go. When I bought them all new clothes and other items at the mall, he reacted negatively again, telling me that my son's new "sandals are for fags" and "kids don't wear shorts on a farm." He put a negative spin on everything, as though baiting me to argue with him — like he actually enjoyed it.

It came to a point where I was so confused, so drained of energy. I tiptoed around him as though on eggshells all of the time. I was nervous going to work during the day in case he made derogatory comments about me to the children in my absence; I was uncomfortable at home in case something I did or didn't do provoked yet another argument. There seemed to be no degree between rage and tenderness with him. Each time he was angry, he would react in the same manner, saying it was obvious that I didn't want to be with him, so I should leave. At times, he would block me from exiting the room we were in, throw things, or slam cupboards to emphasize his hurt. I have to say, I found it all very intimidating.

Sometimes when we were together, the hairs would stand up on the back of my neck for no cognizant reason. I was just very unsettled in his presence. For example, one evening, we had an argument before he was about to leave for his night shift. As I stood in front of the kitchen window, washing the supper dishes, I could see him pacing outside beside his truck, restlessly kicking up dirt with his boots on each turn. Uneasy at the sight of him, I dried my hands and went to the back door to lock up for the night — something I usually did awhile *after* he had gone to work. I turned the bolt to lock it, then looked down at the door handle to lock that. When I looked back up again, Bryan's face suddenly appeared in the window, startling me half to death. I heard him grumble, "Locking me out of my own house?" from outside, and I immediately opened the door for him to come back in. I was trembling. I'm not exactly sure why. I suppose he'd simply forgotten something in the bedroom, because he went in there for a moment before leaving the house for good. But the whole scene made me really nervous. It's hard to explain. He just seemed like a bomb ticking away.

There were nights like that one when I would lie awake in our bed, so exhausted, yet unable to close my eyes. I felt paranoid and unsure of the situation, but not yet ready to leave. Sometimes I wished he would just hit me and get it over with. Other times, I told myself, "Relax. You're overreacting." My mind would spin around like that until I was tired enough to sleep but it was never a refreshing slumber. After awhile, I felt so bogged down that I could barely function during the days.

Finally, out of frustration and growing fear, I demanded marriage counselling as a last resort. I wanted to somehow get through to him that I loved him, but I wasn't going to change every part of my personality just to please him. There had to be a happy medium we could both accept. He went to one session with me, but when I asked that we continue attending, he was furious, arguing that I was "damaging the sacred bond between a husband and wife" by bringing someone else into our private life. For the umpteenth time, he threatened, "If you don't want to be here, go!" so I finally agreed I *would*. There are only so many times a person can be told to leave before they do. And yet, even though he was the one who kept insisting I pack up and go, the realization that I actually would seemed to anger him even more. The next thing I knew, he was threatening *physical* abuse — warning me that if he found me asleep in our bed when he returned from his night shift, he would push me out of it and tear the sheets right off me.

Something in me snapped then. I sat there limp on our couch and watched in disbelief as he raged on, more threats spewing from his mouth when the others didn't produce whatever reaction he was looking for: first, he was going to "run outside right now and tell the children" that I was leaving him; next, he was going to tell everyone at our workplace; then, he was going to start packing up all my things and throw them outside. My voice was calm as I warned him I would not tolerate any more of these threats, but I was shaken and felt sick in the pit of my stomach. All I kept thinking was how on earth had I gotten myself and my son into this mess? I knew we were on our way out. Still, I had no idea how to leave or where to go.

Bryan left for work that night as usual, not actually having made good on his threat to tell the children anything about our fight. I ran a bath for myself and washed away my smeared make-up so the kids wouldn't notice I'd been crying when they came inside. An hour or two later, as anticipated, I received Bryan's standard emotional apology by telephone. If I promised to stay, he would go back to counselling for his drinking and anger. I had to give him one more chance, he said.

I gave him the benefit of the doubt. Again. We had these two children to consider. I also didn't want to admit to all the skeptics that they were right after only five short months of marriage. How humiliating. I suppose at the time the pain of leaving, of facing others with the premature failure of my marriage, still weighed more than the pain of remaining where I was. But that would only last another week.

One morning before work, my son told me that his stomach had been bothering him off and on for the past two weeks. Concerned, I wanted to take him to the medi-clinic that evening to make sure there was nothing seriously wrong. Just a precautionary measure. Not an unreasonable thing to do, you'd think. And yet when I discussed this with Bryan on the phone that afternoon, I was met with resistance just as I had been with so many other things. Rather than simply comforting me or saying, "Well, I'm sure everything is fine, but take him if it'll make you feel better," he impatiently insisted there was no need to go. After a few minutes arguing over this minute detail, I finally put my foot down and said it was not up for discussion. I'd given up the golf lessons, and compromised and rearranged my life to please so many of his other whims. This one was not negotiable. This was my son's health.

When I returned home after work, and an hour-long commute, I immediately called out to my son and told him to get ready. It would be another long drive back to the clinic in the city. I was in our bedroom getting changed when Bryan entered in a huff, displeased by the fact that I was ruining dinner by leaving right away. When that argument didn't dissuade me from going, he changed his angle again. It wasn't the dinner that upset him then; it was the fact that my son and I were going to this clinic *alone*. It was as though now that we were married we had to do everything together or else I had ulterior motives. He actually accused me of trying to separate our family, our children. It was so bizarre. I just shook my head and continued getting ready.

Bryan began his usual ranting and raving about how, if I didn't want to be in this marriage, I could leave at any time I wanted to. I replied, "I'm getting really tired of that threat," and asked him to keep his voice down for the children's sakes. Offended, he flung open our bedroom door, exclaiming that he was "so tired of the shit." As he stormed down the hallway, our children were both in clear view, in their respective bedrooms across the way, both with their doors open. They were listening in on our argument.

I wanted to leave quickly to avoid any further confrontation in front of the kids, but before I could get my shoes on, Bryan was back in the bedroom and at me again, this time leaving our door wide open. When I tried to ignore him rather than fuelling the argument, he went berserk and walked out into the centre of the hallway between the children's bedrooms, yelling, "I want a divorce! Do you hear what I'm saying to you?! I'm asking you for a divorce!" All I remember is watching his daughter's jaw drop open before collecting my purse, my son, his GameBoy, and then walking out. That's all we had with us, but I didn't care — we weren't going back. Bryan's behaviour had now escalated from *threatening* to involve our children to *involving* them. I felt it was only a matter of time before he made good on his other threats, too.

We spent the next five days in hotels in the city while I arranged movers and storage for our belongings, a new place to live, an RCMP escort back to the farm to retrieve our things, and a lawyer to obtain a restraining order. It was a frightening time. All of our belongings were still at the farm. I had no idea if Bryan was going through my things or destroying them as he'd done with the photo album. I figured he was probably capable of anything at that point. He also continued phoning my cell phone eight and nine times a day, trying to locate us and bring us home. This freaked me out even more. Everywhere I went, I was afraid of running into him so, I grouped all of my summer holidays at work and used them early. I intended to keep as low a profile as possible while making these arrangements.

Finally, I was able to get a short-term ex-parte restraining order, but that didn't stop Bryan from contacting my mother — a strict violation of his terms. And after a month or two of battling through lawyers, he was able to have the restraining order set aside. According to our laws here, emotional abuse is not enough to warrant a long-term restraining order. After all, I left before he had opportunity to *hit* me, so the judge didn't seem to think my physical safety was in any jeopardy. Never mind our *emotional* safety.

Sure enough, with the restraining order gone, Bryan was back to phoning my cellular very soon after. One night, I finally answered it. I guess I was tired of going through lawyers and the courts; I wanted to tell him myself how angry I was. And that's how the conversation began ... with me saying it was over and asking him to leave me alone. But somewhere along the way, I began to sympathize with his tears and his apologies. My heart began to ache for him. Somewhere along the way, I agreed to meet him at a neutral location — a restaurant — to give him a "proper good-bye." I don't understand, still, how I could go from being afraid enough to pay thousands of dollars to keep a restraining order in place, to agreeing to meet with him and talk. Even more, I don't understand how we ended up in an embrace ... and then back at the farm, making love, discussing the possibility of reconciliation. But that's what happened that night. And it still has me so confused.

As ridiculous as this probably sounds after everything I've told you, I felt so drawn to him that night at the restaurant. I still do as I write this. He keeps phoning, keeps saying how sorry he is, and that he realizes everything he did wrong. He insists he has continued in therapy since I left him and that he sees everything more clearly now. I didn't give him the opportunity to get help before I left, but he's getting that help now. He says if I just try and give him one more honest chance, I'll be able to see all these changes for myself.

I probably wouldn't have even given him the time of day, let alone agreed to meet with him that night, had I not been back to see our marriage counsellor on my own a day or two prior. When I went to meet with her, I expected that she would support my decision to leave; and yet, I got the distinct impression she didn't think his behaviour was all that bad. I asked her, "Since when is burning someone's personal property, throwing things at them, and threatening to push them out of their bed *normal*?" And yet she seemed to imply that I'd reacted too rashly by filing for divorce. She recommended I consider a "healing separation" instead.

I haven't given Bryan my new address or phone number (it is unlisted) and I haven't seen him in person again since that night last week. But, in light of my conversation with the marriage counsellor, and our intimate evening together, I have agreed to hear him out, talk to him on my cell phone once a week, and possibly return to couple's therapy with him. However, I've asked that the children not be involved at this time. My son seems to be getting on with things okay. I don't want to disrupt that. And Bryan's daughter? I don't know.

So, what are your thoughts? What the hell am I doing? Am I wasting my time? Can he change? Will he change? I'm so confused by everything. Did I get this all wrong as the marriage counsellor seems to have implied?

Help.

----- Original Message -----
From: Someone Who Cares

To: Katlyn
Sent: Tuesday, August 20, 11:56 AM
Subject: Re: Help

Hi Katlyn,

No matter what the courts say, emotional abuse is just as traumatic as physical. After all, physical bruises heal, but what about the bruises on your soul and your heart? I truly believe that the courts should give emotional abuse the attention it deserves.

With regard to your marriage counsellor, my advice would be to trust your own instincts. If you feel, deep down, she doesn't understand your circumstances, then listen to that; trust in that. Call your local police station's domestic conflict unit or a local shelter and have them refer you to someone else who *does* understand. Too many times, I've seen this same situation. Many counsellors are trained to look for a cause (you) and effect (abuse) in relationships. They don't understand that both verbal and physical abuse come from the same underlying control issues, and that neither is excusable. Your marriage counsellor has been trained to believe all relationship issues result from communication problems, but that's not always the case. In an abusive relationship, you are not starting out on the same level. It is the abuser who holds the control and manipulates the situation.

I can't tell you for certain whether or not Bryan has changed. But I can tell you that counselling and therapy will not work for an abuser unless they are totally willing to change. If he is at all reluctant to change, or in denial of his behaviour altogether, then therapy will do nothing for him, at least not provide any long-term results. And "healing separations" do not work in abusive situations, because the continued contact only allows for continued control tactics.

It sounds like Bryan is very controlling and that the emotional abuse has quickly escalated. No one deserves that. You have the opportunity to decide what is best for you and your son, and that is what you should do. Marriage is a commitment that should be upheld, but not at the expense of your individuality, happiness, or safety. Always remember that.

The best advice I can offer you is this: think of all the times he has made you feel bad and ask yourself if it is worth it. If you go back, and this continues, will you be able to get away as easily next time? Also, do you think that you could be happier without him? Life is too short and there are too many people in this world to settle for emotional abuse and heartache. If I were in your situation, I would stay away and move on with my life. But I can't make that decision for you. Listen to your gut.

The likelihood that he will change is not good, Katlyn. Most abusers find ways to hide their abusive tendencies for short periods of time in order to gain back the trust of their victims (called the honeymoon phase), but it usually doesn't last. Bryan could be a rare exception to this rule. It is possible, but very unlikely.

My advice to you is to give it more time. Keep your distance from him. Tell him you want your space and that you will let him know if or when you're ready to resume your relationship. See how he reacts. If he has truly changed, he will understand and be supportive. If, however, he seems to be impatient and pressures you, that should answer your question. Watch his behaviour closely right now. If you feel he has not completely changed then stay away.

I hope my advice has helped you a little. Please don't hesitate to email me again if you have any other questions or need more advice. Take care.

Lots of love to you.

----- Original Message -----
From: Katlyn
To: Someone Who Cares
Sent: Wednesday, August 21, 7:04 PM
Subject: Re: Help

Thank you for responding to my email so quickly. Your guidance comes at a time when I need it like never before. I have a couple of other things I want your opinion on ...

Three incidents occurred during our marriage that I didn't write about earlier, as they aren't really *tangible* sorts of abuse. Maybe they aren't abuse at all. Maybe I'm overreacting as Bryan has accused me of many times. But I'd still like your opinion:

The first incident happened on our very first day as a married couple. When we got back home to the farm, we were all sitting on the deck together, chatting. Bryan's dad was there, along with my brothers, mom, and our kids. We were laughing about a day not long before. That day, Bryan had chopped the head off one of his chickens in front of me to show me what happens to its body afterward. I cringed at the thought of it, and we were all laughing about this episode, about the fact that I've been somewhat sheltered when it comes to country living. Until then, the only chicken I'd seen was pre-packaged in the grocery store. Anyway, that's when Bryan made this rather unsettling joke. In reference to that particular chicken's fate, he added, "Now Katlyn knows what'll happen to her if she ever tries to leave me." We all chuckled at the time. It seemed innocent enough. But I'll admit, I was bothered by it.

There was another day when Bryan and I were driving into the city together. My cell phone was sitting between us, and, when he noticed the message "One Missed Call" on its screen, he seemed bothered, preoccupied. He said, "You know, cell phones are perfect for people who are having affairs. They would never call their lover from home. They'd use their cell instead." I figured he must be joking, so I joked along with him about my supposed "affair" via my cell phone, but I have to say it was a very bizarre and uncomfortable conversation. It was as though he was testing me.

There was another time when I had read this horrendous account of an East-Indian woman whose husband had accused her of having an affair — an affair she didn't even have — and he brutally beat her. He strung her upside down by her feet, hit her, slashed off her ears and nose with a knife, leaving her for dead. She ended up surviving the ordeal and this article presented her life as a survivor. Anyway, I was really bothered by it, and I brought it up with Bryan, expecting him to agree that it was a disturbing article — like everyone else I'd talked to about it. But he was removed from emotion. His only comment was, "I don't know what I'd be capable of if you ever cheated on me." *That* was unsettling. I sat with that for a few days before bringing it up with him again, asking him why he would say such a thing. He just chuckled and remarked, "Oh, Katlyn. You take everything so literally," as though I had made a mountain out of a molehill. So I let it go.

What do you think about all this? Sick sense of humour? Or something more?

Hope to hear from you soon,
Katlyn

----- Original Message -----
From: Someone Who Cares
To: Katlyn
Sent: Thursday, August 22, 10:12 AM
Subject: Re: Help

Hi again Katlyn,

I can see how each one of these incidents can be taken as abusive. I can't necessarily tell you whether or not they were meant that way, because I don't know Bryan. But I can tell you they can easily be taken either way. From everything else you've emailed me about him, I feel those situations were probably his method of testing you, seeing where you would draw the line.

Usually, when someone with abusive tendencies gets involved in a relationship, they test the waters. They make small comments here and there to see exactly how much they can get away with. If certain comments get really negative responses, they know to back off. I think he probably came to the conclusion that you would tolerate these comments, thus opening the door for more intense comments. I know that really doesn't seem fair because, in a new relationship, most people tolerate a little more than they normally would, just because the relationship is new.

It is really hard to spot an abusive personality in the first few days, weeks, or months of a relationship, because you're just testing each other out. What's funny is that even now, after all my training and personal experience with abuse, I still have a hard time spotting an abusive person. Sometimes they are really obvious; but mostly, they are just like everyone else — except they have a totally different personality in private. I wish there was an "abuser alarm" or tool people could have to be warned of such people, but I doubt there will ever be an invention like that, at least not in my lifetime.

My advice to you is to stay strong and stand your ground. If you let him get the upper hand at this time, he'll take it and run. Now is your chance to show him that you aren't going to be treated like this any longer. Either he will respect that or he will get fed up and walk away. Either way, you will win in the end.

Just try to take good care of yourself right now. This is not an easy time, especially when you aren't entirely sure what to think about him. Just take things slowly, and listen to your feelings and instincts. Remember that no one deserves to be treated this way. If you feel that he is still going to hurt you, just walk away. It really isn't worth it.

----- Original Message -----
From: Katlyn
To: Someone Who Cares
Sent: Friday, August 23, 5:43 PM

Subject: Re: Help

Let me tell you some more about Bryan ... and *me* for
that matter. Then I'd like your absolute, honest, gut
instinct on this situation. Mine is still too clouded. I'm so
depressed and I'm missing the person I married, hoping
he still exists. Maybe he never did. I'm so confused.

During one of my first dates with Bryan, I learned he that
had a daughter and was a single parent. Her mother, his
first wife "Carol," had died something like eight years prior.
Friends at work had told me beforehand that she'd
committed suicide, although I didn't ask him about this at
the time. I didn't feel it was my place to pry.

I remember feeling quite comfortable with him in the
beginning, as though I'd met someone I could truly relate
to — for two reasons: first, when I was sixteen, my
father shot himself after a rather serious bout of
depression (an illness he'd struggled with off and on for
years); and, second, I became a single parent at the
age of twenty after my son's father and I separated.
Depression and suicide are still fairly taboo in our society.
Few people understand the illness. And so to finally meet
someone who had been through something similar, also
someone who was a single parent like me ... I felt such an
affinity with Bryan. I thought I'd finally met the one person
who could understand where I was coming from, because
he was coming from the same place.

As I got to know him a bit better, I learned that his first
marriage to Carol had been rough. He told me that she'd
had some rare illness and no one knew exactly how to
treat her for it. Instead, they pumped her full of all
these really toxic, addictive, over-the-counter drugs and
she became dependent on them, among other drugs.
Bryan said they argued constantly. He said the source of
their arguments was her addiction (of course, never
mind *his* drinking). The night she died, they'd had a

huge fight in which he told her to "get the hell out" of their home and get her "shit together," or she would not be allowed back. He explained that he was practicing tough love, so she would get help for her drug problem. But later that night, she was found dead at a friend's house. Sometimes, Bryan says it was an intentional overdose; other times, he says she was already so toxic from all the drugs that, when she took her regular prescription, she simply went into organ failure. It's hard to know what really happened because his story seems to vary. Then again, how can anyone ever know? Carol is no longer here to defend herself or tell us her side of the story.

I didn't hold Carol's tragedy against him. As I said before, a loved one of mine did the same, and I don't think people should hold *that* against me. Also, it seemed entirely reasonable to me that Bryan was practising tough love with her. If she was a drug addict, I thought tough love was probably warranted. That's why I excused it and didn't question it further. If anything, having lived through a similar trauma, I thought maybe I could help Bryan find closure. Whenever he talked about Carol's suicide, or their arguments, or that his parents had had a couple violent rows of their own during his childhood, he seemed like a wounded animal in need of sympathy. I suppose it brought out the protective side of me. Of course, I didn't actually see any of these arguments for myself. I'm just going by what he told me.

Bryan's mother passed away last year and this was yet another source of pain for him. He and his father appeared to be a couple of jolly guys in the company of others. They quickly accepted us into their family, and we got along very well. Still, they were both pretty heavy drinkers, both still mourning Bryan's mother's death, and they bickered back and forth quite a lot. At the time, I figured it was just their way of relating to one another. It didn't occur to me for a minute that

Bryan's aggression toward his father would one day be directed at me, because everyone at work who knew him had nothing but wonderful things to say. Whenever his name came up in conversation, I always heard, "What a great guy!" so I went with that. And even though both he and his father drank a fair amount, neither of them ever appeared drunk or out of control. Never. So, I decided the bickering and the drinking were minor flaws I could live with. If Bryan could accept that I smoked cigarettes, I could accept his beer. It's all about give and take, acceptance of each other's flaws, right? There's no such thing as perfection, but this seemed close enough for me. I thought I was in love. I thought he loved me, too.

All through our engagement, Bryan and I spoke very openly and honestly about everything. Or, so it seemed. I questioned his drinking, but he assured me it was not a problem. He claimed that it had never taken precedence over his family or finances. Looking at his daughter, who seemed well adjusted and polite, visiting his beautiful farm, and knowing he'd held the same job for several years, I thought to myself: That seems entirely true. I didn't want to judge him, you know? Maybe the reason so many of my past relationships had failed was because I'd been too critical of those men, or focused more on the negatives rather than the positives. I didn't want to make that same mistake with Bryan, and risk losing who might actually be "the one" for me.

Bryan said he'd been on a few dates between the death of his first wife and meeting me, but that was it. He could never stay attracted to anyone, let alone fall in love again until he met me. He told me he'd never loved anyone as much as me — not even Carol — and he seemed very genuine in saying this. I believed him. I *wanted* to believe him. No one had ever made me feel as special before.

I know it sounds naïve to say that I knew this person well enough to marry him after only five months. But that's the way it seemed. I didn't hold anything back from him. At the age of thirty, I felt I knew what I wanted and where I was going in life. I'd experienced enough through dating, career changes, and life in general by then to have a very strong sense of who I was. I shared *everything* with him and he related so well. Add to that the fact that he had his daughter and a father, and I had my son and a mother — it was as though we were the missing pieces to each other's puzzle. It felt meant to be, like we were soul mates. And so I held on to that. I really wanted that dream to be real.

I anticipated bumps in the road, particularly in our first year as we adjusted to our new family. But I predicted *nothing* as deep as the potholes we hit. So, when all of these problems started happening, when it all started going so wrong so quickly, I wondered, "What did I miss here? Why didn't I see this all coming?" I felt like such a fool. I've never felt more hurt or ashamed in all of my life. I still can't quite believe it. Separated in *less* than six months? I never want to show my face again!

Now you have pretty much all of the information I have. What's your honest take on all this? Am I overreacting? Or should I have known better in the first place?

Katlyn

----- Original Message -----
From: Someone Who Cares
To: Katlyn
Sent: Saturday, August 24, 1:11 PM
Subject: Re: Help

Hi Katlyn,

It sounds like you've thought a lot about this situation and I think that's the best approach. It seems to me that no one will ever really know what happened to Carol. Your guess is probably as good as anyone's. But perhaps one thing to ponder is this: how much of her drug use was linked to dealing with the illness and how much of it was to connected to dealing with Bryan? Remember, people like Bryan like to use different reasoning and excuses for their behaviour such as: Carol was sick and we fought over her medications; my parents argued regularly during my childhood, so that's how I grew up; et cetera. They displace the blame rather than taking responsibility for their own actions.

My gut instinct in cases such as this is to follow my *only* instinct in cases such as this: if he hurts you, stay away. And I have to say the fact that he's told you his parents had a couple "violent rows" during his upbringing does raise a red flag. Everyone has their arguments, Katlyn; it is a natural element to human interaction. The red flag in these situations is a history of violent behaviour within an abuser's family, or a violent history of his own (such as smashing beer bottles against the wall next to you). In many instances, you were not the first victim and you may not be the last.

Let me ask you something: by following your gut instinct, have you truly seen any change in him? A change that is substantial would be evident before you even stepped foot on that farm again. How does he talk to you on the phone? Does it seem like he is just trying to be nice or that he genuinely cares? It's hard to know after being together for such a short amount of time. The fact is, you fell in love and moved too quickly. It's not a crime — I can testify to that. But it does prevent you from learning more about the environment and the past of the man you plan to share the rest of your life with. Marriage is a huge step. Many people take that step too quickly, not realizing the full weight of their commitment. But people are going to do what they want, right?

Still, sometimes giving all of these feelings time to process is the best way to handle the situation. If you're unsure, then give him time to prove himself. Talk on the phone if you must, but, until you're completely sure, don't spend anymore time alone with him. Don't go to his farm and don't let him know where you live. You must keep the homes separate at this point.

Most abusers are patient when it comes to waiting for their potential victim to "come around." The key here is that you do not tell him your motives. Don't give him any indication of time limits that you have set for him or yourself. If he knows he only has to behave for two weeks, then he can manage. But if he has no idea how long he has to keep playing nice, the truth will come out soon enough.

Recovering from abuse has a lot to do with waiting: waiting for that feeling of safety to return, waiting for that feeling of love to return, waiting for that feeling of self-worth again. If you don't have those feelings when you are with him — of safety, love, and self-worth — then leave him in the dust and move on.

Another thought for you: I know both your children are young, but did they understand any of what was going on? Does your son appear to have a particular opinion about Bryan or the marriage? If you don't know, ask him. Sometimes a child's interpretation of a situation is fairly accurate. They haven't experienced the influences of society that create biased judgments (don't you wish we could maintain that ability as adults). So, ask his opinion and listen to his response. You never know.

Overall, just take your time and don't allow Bryan to pressure you. If you don't feel completely comfortable with him, then don't go back. That is my gut feeling and my advice to you, but, in the end, it all depends on your own gut feeling, Katlyn. Trust in your own instincts.

I hope that this insight helps you. I know how hard these feelings are to handle, and I know how hard this decision is for you to make. I know because I was in your position too many times in the past. Just don't allow yourself to be hurt or go back to a situation that you know in your heart to be dangerous. Just be safe, okay?

----- Original Message -----
From: Katlyn
To: Someone Who Cares
Sent: Saturday, August 24, 6:24 PM
Subject: Re: Help

No, I can't say that I sense a substantial change in him. I feel as pressured as I did before the wedding, and there are still those little nondescript contradictions in the things he says and does. Maybe in his own Bryan way, he genuinely cares for me, but he is being overly sugary and apologetic right now. And he does seem impatient, phoning me at all hours of the day.

As for the children and their perspective, I haven't had any contact with his daughter since I left, other than writing her a letter and mailing it to their neighbour's farm. In it, I told her not to let anyone else try to tell her how I feel about her — I'm the only one who can tell her, and I feel love, respect, and admiration. I told her that I couldn't take her with me because she's not my legal daughter. I didn't make any direct reference to her father other than to say that she's been through a few things in her life already (including the loss of her mother and grandmother), and this is going to be another one of those things. But I told her that her strength will get her through this experience, as it did the other times.

Bryan's daughter is a real sweetheart, a real "pleaser" with adults. I remember one time, sitting at the dinner table with the children. I don't recall the exact context of our conversation, but she said, "My dad only drinks four or five beers a day."

I corrected her with, "No. He drinks more than that." Nothing else was said.

Nothing was ever said (on my part, anyway) in front of the kids. We didn't talk about things because I didn't want to badmouth Bryan in front of them. I didn't want to involve them or let them know what was going on behind closed doors. But I do know they heard yelling ...

I know this because, on the night I left, right after Bryan had yelled "I want a divorce!" in front them, my son and I had a little talk in the car. When I told him we weren't going back, he began to cry and admitted he'd heard yelling before. I said, "I know that. And you're not going to hear it anymore. I don't want you to live somewhere where you have to hear things like 'I want a divorce!' and yelling every other day. That's not fair."

In response to the rest of your email, the fact that you've dealt with these emotions "too many times" in your life tells me that you went back. A few times. And it never did change. Was yours also the whirlwind romance as described on your website? That description sent shivers down my spine, because before I'd even gone to the website, I'd been explaining my emotions to friends. I compared my feelings to being caught up in a tornado, and said I felt very dizzy from all the spinning. Bryan also meets about ninety percent of the rest of the abuser profile. It was very unnerving to read.

I guess the reason I'm most torn is because there are children involved. If there were no children, I think I would go back, give him the chance to really prove himself, try to help him in any way I could. After all, I married him. And if it didn't change the second time around, so what? I'm the only one being hurt. But in our case, there are these two kids who have already been hurt once. Do I risk hurting them again? And do I risk letting my son grow up with the same upbringing Bryan had — with the alcohol and the arguing? That doesn't feel fair at all anymore. Right now, my son seems to be doing fine. To disrupt that again makes me very uneasy.

In one of Bryan's voice mails the other night, he told me that his daughter is devastated over this, wondering why this keeps happening to her, why she keeps losing her moms. But then, in the next breath, he said something like, "You know kids. They're the strong ones. They put on the happy face." So, it's hard to know how she is for sure.

Is it my responsibility to be there to help "Bryan?" And should I hold myself responsible for his daughter? Yes, I was her mother, I suppose ... but for a very short time. I don't feel I was given enough of an opportunity to really become her mother in the full sense of that word. So, is she truly my responsibility here? Should I be blaming myself that she's been hurt, as I have? I know I walked out on her. Do I owe it to her to go back, with the chance of walking out on her again? How do you handle the kids in a situation like this? Should I call her?

----- Original Message -----
From: Someone Who Cares
To: Katlyn
Sent: Saturday, August 24, 10:05 PM
Subject: Re: Help

Hey again Katlyn.

I could write a novel on my experience with abusive relationships. Yes, I did go back many times, because I thought I loved him and that he loved me. I can't say for sure if that was really true in either case, but I now know that there's no point in trying to find the answer. It's over.

When I wrote the first version of the website content, I based a lot of my examples and information on my own personal experiences. My relationship with "Aaron" was not nearly as bad as some of the other stories I've heard from people I have counselled through this site. But it was bad enough. The whirlwind feelings and the honeymoon syndrome were both big reasons I stayed as long as I did. I was fortunate enough not to have had children during this time, so I was really only hurting myself. Although the abuse was partly physical, it was primarily emotional. For example, one night I was on the phone with Aaron. We had an argument and I ended up telling him that I didn't want to see him again. Still on the phone, he grabbed a knife and stabbed himself while I listened. Needless to say, I was terrified whenever I tried to leave him, because there was always the chance of another suicide attempt. It happened more than once, I can tell you that.

Day by day, it seems the memories of him get foggier. I know that's for the best. He was sentenced to jail for sexually assaulting me and two other women. Since then, I haven't heard a word from him — and that's fine by me. Those years we were together changed me; I would like to think for the better, because I now devote myself to helping others in similar situations.

Whoa, I really went off there, didn't I? Sorry for venting. Here I am trying to help you and give you advice and I just about wrote a novel!

As for the rest of your email, I know it is hard to deal with this type of situation when children are involved. I have a young daughter, so I know how hard it is to want to protect your child but to also want to return to a potentially dangerous situation. If your son seems well adjusted and doesn't seem to mind the change, that's a good thing. Going back and forth repeatedly will only make things harder on him. Remember that. As for hurting Bryan's daughter, I really can't say anything to make that decision easier except this: she will heal. She is *his* daughter and, although I know you don't want to just abandon her, she is *his* responsibility — not yours. If you decide to go back, don't do it simply for her. She is still young and will recover. Kids are amazingly resilient, of that I am sure.

You should take care of your son right now and let Bryan take care of his daughter. I know you care about her and want her to be happy, but I am sure that she also cares for you. She probably would not want you to return at the expense of your happiness. She might not understand that now, but she will. Eventually, she will be old enough to discern her father's faults for herself. But that's not your immediate concern. Just focus on your own son and happiness.

It is a whole new ball game once you have children. When you make the decision to return or to stay away, you have to make the decision with your son in mind — not just yourself. Remember that abusive tendencies, especially verbal and emotional abuse, will eventually be passed on to children. Bryan is only focussing his abuse toward you for now, but, as the children get older, he may start directing abuse toward them. Males pick up these tendencies more easily than females, and, with your son being in that environment, he might grow up to handle family in the same way. The alcoholism might also be picked up. Just a few things for you to think about.

My opinion must be obvious by now. But, then again, don't let my personal opinion sway you if you feel I'm wrong. The decision is ultimately yours to make, and I'm here to support you no matter what you decide.

Good luck to you. Please keep me posted on how things are going.

----- Original Message -----
From: Katlyn
To: Someone Who Cares
Sent: Sunday, August 25, 10:39 AM
Subject: Re: Help

Don't ever feel that you have to apologize for "venting" to me about your own experience. You're a human being, too. And reading your story, knowing I'm not the only one who has experienced something like this, is so helpful. My head is so much clearer than it was a week ago, a month ago. I suppose my gut knew all along I should leave him, but I needed time to be able to trust that feeling. Thank you for all your patience while I worked through this.

I told a friend of mine that if Bryan's daughter takes anything good from this situation, I hope she learns that she doesn't have to stay in a bad marriage. Throughout her upbringing, she's seen women stay. So, maybe now, after having met me, she'll see that there is another way. Even if she's mad at me right now, I hope this lesson stays with her. I hope I'm an influence if and when she enters a similar relationship. That's all I can hope for.

The sad thing about all this is Bryan. I can't help feeling sorry for him. I don't think he means to hurt others, but he simply doesn't know any better, due to having seen his own parents argue during his upbringing. And the alcohol only adds to the problem. He's been drinking for years. He's always been around alcohol, so I don't know how he'll ever be able to stop, even if he wants to. That's so sad, because he really does have some good qualities. He obviously can't see them in himself.

----- Original Message -----
From: Someone Who Cares
To: Katlyn
Sent: Sunday, August 25, 9:53 PM
Subject: Re: Help

Katlyn,

You are very welcome. I am always here if you need someone to talk to.

In response to your last paragraph, I can see how easy it could be to feel sorry for Bryan, but don't let that be an excuse to take him back. So often, abusers solicit sympathy in this way. They blame their parents for their actions and, although it's true that parents influence a person's behaviour, it is not an excuse. Abusers need to take responsibility. I don't care how horrible their parents were, they are still accountable for their own actions. As for the alcohol, abusers often use it as yet another excuse for their behaviour, but it's not. While it's true that alcohol and drugs often go hand in hand with abuse, they are still separate issues. Alcoholism doesn't make someone abuse; it just makes the abuse worse.

I am sure that Bryan has some really great qualities. If he didn't, you wouldn't have become involved with him. However, it comes to a point when you have to decide whether the good qualities really compensate for the bad. I know in my own situation, the reason that I went back as many times as I did was because of those great qualities. But then my ex tried to convince me that he had cancer, which was a lie. And he put a gun to his head during another argument. That's when I finally realized that those good qualities could never outweigh the bad. It is a hard decision to make, but one we all have to at some point.

I am glad that I was able to clear up these feelings for you. I hope that the advice I have given you will help you see this through to the end. If you ever need more advice or just want to share stories or vent, I am here. After all, that's what the website was built for — to try to help people.

* * *

Once I finally came to the decision to end my marriage for good, I thought the worst was surely over. Although I was swamped with debt from staying at hotels, moving expenses, and lawyers, I tried to count my blessings. I still had my career, my son and I were safe, and we had all of our belongings back. Even better, we had a new place to live in the city. Now it would simply be a matter of finalizing divorce legalities, healing, and moving on, right? Wrong. It had only just begun ...

Bryan didn't know where I lived, nor did he have my home phone number, but he knew where I worked because he worked for the same company. Just as had been the case both before and during our marriage, this man was not about to take no for an answer. His campaign of stalking me at the workplace escalated.

I tried everything humanly possible to get through to Bryan that it was over between us. I was as compassionate as I could be. But, when taking his calls myself, I seemed only to unwittingly lead him on. So I tried another approach — asking his therapist to reason with him on my behalf. Even that didn't resolve the issue. Nor did my final, forceful telephone conversation with him a couple of weeks later. Nor did hanging up on him when he called after that.

By September, Bryan was leaving me an unbearable twenty or more voice mails a week at the office — at all hours of the day. To make matters worse, he was leaving countless letters and gifts on my desk during his night shifts. Every morning when I got to work, I was bombarded with this negativity. Sometimes, the calls and letters were romantic. Other times, they were remorseful or upset, warning me that he would never give me this divorce. There was nothing explicitly threatening in them, but his constant presence in my life drained my energy.

I decided that if a restraining order, and pleas from me and his therapist had not gotten through to him, perhaps the best approach would be avoidance. I stopped answering my phones altogether; instead, letting each call ring through to voice mail to separate client messages from Bryan's. I deleted all of his voice mails with the rationale that if I didn't listen to them, he couldn't affect me. I mailed several of his letters and gifts back to his divorce lawyer, telling myself that *she* would reason with him and he'd eventually give up this campaign of harassment. I even asked office management to speak to him, thinking he would surely listen to his superiors. *Still*, he persisted. Nothing was working and I was growing increasingly confused. Should I view this as unconditional love or as obsessive, controlling behaviour? And if it was chivalry, why did it make me so upset? None of it made any sense.

Most disturbing was a day in late October when Bryan had a bouquet of roses delivered to me at work. I placed them on the desk in his office, unopened, as yet another strong indicator that I wished to be left alone. The next morning, I returned to the office only to find them back on my desk. He'd propped them up against the wall for all to see, the wrapping paper around them torn open, with a letter attached angrily exclaiming, "These were given to you out of love!" I felt like I was losing control of my life, like I would never be free of this man. This drained my vitality even more.

Enough was enough, so I called the city police for advice. The good news? They might be able to help me. The bad news? They requested I meet with them to present my *evidence*. Because I'd deleted all of his messages and mailed the letters and gifts back to his divorce lawyer, I did not have any evidence to show. I had another unbearable week to endure, during which time I collected twenty-seven more voice mails and a dozen new letters. Then, I called the police back to book an appointment.

After we met, the police issued Bryan a telephoned warning to make him very aware that I was feeling harassed and he should leave me alone. For a month, there were no more phone calls, letters, or gifts. I thought perhaps this nightmare was finally over, perhaps Bryan had taken the threat of a criminal harassment charge seriously. But just when I'd come to a point where I was beginning to feel relief, the phone calls started again. It wasn't over yet.

Up to this point, I had been wary of Bryan. I felt exhausted from the harassment and concerned for my emotional safety. It was as though I was always looking over my shoulder, waiting for the next thing to happen. But now I feared for my physical safety, as well, just as I had toward the end of our marriage. Although none of his messages or actions were overtly threatening, it was the implication of his relentless pursuit that frightened me the most. He would clearly stop at nothing to get to me, even after several warnings from a judge, lawyers, and now the police. I knew these were not the actions of a rational person, and I seriously questioned his stability.

More voice mails, letters, and gifts at my workplace followed. And then came the day when he showed up unexpectedly during my shift. When I saw him down the corridor, I immediately grabbed my coat to leave the building, but he called after me as he followed closely behind, all the way up to the front security desk. He stood only 8 feet away, watching me as I reported him to security. He actually stood there and *watched* me report him. I can't even begin to explain how vulnerable I felt. My mind couldn't help but wander and consider the possible outcomes of this disquieting game. It was a psychological terror that stayed with me from that point onward.

Now it had been ventured beyond the threat of contact by phone or letter. Now the fear of bumping into him had become a reality. And this fear extended beyond the workplace. Whenever I was driving to or from work, I was constantly watching and waiting. Every time I saw a blue truck drive by that remotely resembled Bryan's, my heart rate increased and I felt nauseated. If my doorbell rang when I was not expecting anyone, I would stand paralyzed in fear of who was behind the door. I couldn't eat, my sleeping habits were erratic, and my concentration levels were completely shot. By now, I had dropped twenty pounds from a frame that didn't need to lose ten. I felt that same intense fatigue as when "Abby" attempted suicide fifteen years before.

I lasted only another short week at work after Bryan was finally charged with criminal harassment in late January and a police undertaking was put in place. I knew in my heart that, as long as he was provided access in the workplace, he would take full advantage to assault me further — protection order or not. I also feared that he might become violent, particularly now that he'd been charged. He would be that much more hostile to me.

That's when I ran completely out of steam, fell apart, and went on medical leave. Emotionally, mentally, financially, and physically spent, I could no longer carry on. My body shut down on me. It said enough. Soon after, I was diagnosed with post traumatic stress disorder.

I spent the next two months on self-imposed house arrest, thrashing around inside myself, before finally relenting to the realization that my career was over. I could not return to a building where Bryan continued working, so I felt compelled to resign. This was a career I'd spent several years building; it was the only decent-paying position I'd ever held. It was my final safety net, the one means I thought I had to somehow turn my situation around. And now, adding insult to injury, even it was gone. Bryan had taken everything from me: my home, all of my financial gains, my health, and now my only source of income. All in one year.

He pleaded "Not guilty" to the charge of criminal harassment, so there was another agonizing seven-month wait for his trial. During that time, I kept an eagle eye on my public affairs to prevent Bryan from finding out where I was. My entire life hung in the balance. As the trial date drew near, there was a tremendous buildup of emotion: the anticipation of a hostile courtroom and intrusive cross-examination; all of the mental preparation as I rehearsed my testimony over and over again inside my head. And then the day finally came. But the trial had to be *adjourned* due to improper disclosure of evidence between the Crown Prosecutor's office and the defense attorney. Most infuriating was the knowledge they'd had seven months to prepare, including a preliminary hearing in which they were supposed to have compared their files to prevent this very thing from happening. And yet, no one caught this discrepancy until a week before the trial. I left the courthouse completely deflated.

Discouraged as I was, I learned a valuable lesson that day. I could no longer allow my life to revolve around this endless bureaucracy. I had to believe that Bryan was no longer my problem, either; his fate now rested in the hands of the courts. For months, I'd been telling myself: When the trial is over, I'll quit smoking. When the trial is over, I'll start exercising and eating right again. When the trial is over, I'll finally sit down and write that letter to my son. But now the trial had been postponed for another eight months. Was I supposed to continue living in limbo until then, knowing it may very well be delayed yet again? I decided NO. If I did, I would only be hurting myself even more.

When I began writing Calvin's letter, I still didn't know what the final outcome to this story would be. I decided it was irrelevant anyway. Deep down, I knew that what Bryan had done to my life was a serious crime, whether a judge would later determine this or not. I also knew that my most important focus should be my new marketing position with another company, rebuilding our lives, and trying to find what I had gained from this experience rather than dwelling on what I'd lost.

What I'd gained was knowledge. Compassion. After my own experience with domestic abuse, I've often found myself wondering about that woman, Cindy, who lived down our old block in Calgary. I now understand how easily someone can be manipulated by another, how a person can go from love, to fear, back to love in a heartbeat. Especially if the abuser persists, and knows exactly what to say. It's a strange and powerful phenomenon: the way abuse can alter your perceptions, wear you down to the point where you doubt your own God-given instincts, and allow yourself to be hurt time and again. I know how completely drained *I* felt after living with Bryan for a mere five and a half months, so I can only imagine how someone must feel after several years in that kind of home. Even with all the resources I had at my disposal — vehicle, cell phone, my own career, my own bank account, a supportive family, and the knowledge that I could live independently as I had before — it was still a major struggle to end my relationship with

Bryan. Cindy clearly didn't even have that. Her husband controlled everything. No wonder she stayed.

Emotional and economical barriers are not the only factors that make it difficult to leave. The whole legal process can make you feel as victimized as the abuser did. Every time you are second-guessed or cross-examined, every time the police push your case back due to demanding workloads, or the lawyers request adjournments, it takes another piece from you — until there's simply nothing left to take. You honestly begin to wonder which is worse: remaining in the relationship and being abused by one person; or trying to leave and feeling abused by an entire fleet.

The ignorance in our society can tarnish your faith, too. Whereas Cindy had to deal with my ignorance in the form of rejection, I later dealt with ignorance in the form of denial. In my particular case, because there was no obvious physical violence, no visible proof of the abuse in the form of a black eye or broken bone, it was an uphill climb to convince many that I *was* being hurt. My employer lacked knowledge of the dangers of stalking, and, as a result, enabled it to continue in their building for months — despite my cries for help. It was not until I was completely worn, and Bryan had been charged criminally, that anyone began to see the situation for what it really was. Of course, it was too late by then; I had been forced out of my career. This was very isolating, let me tell you. A very eye-opening experience for me.

I'd like to think all of this has made me more aware and that much wiser than I had been. I've learned that I'm no different from Cindy at all. No matter what, we're all the same, we're all just as vulnerable. I only wish I knew back then what I know now. Maybe I would have stopped to help her just as someone later stopped to help me, instead of throwing her phone number in the garbage and looking the other way. Perhaps then she would have found the strength to move on as I did.

* * *

One week before the second date of his criminal harassment trial, Bryan changed his plea to guilty. After all the waiting and anticipation, I was shocked (relieved!) to know I would not have to step foot in the courtroom after all. A full week passed before I finally believed it was true. It was over. Thank God it was over.

At his sentencing hearing, Bryan was convicted of criminal harassment contrary to section 264(2)(b) of the Criminal Code of Canada. He received a conditional discharge plus a one-year probation period. This meant there were certain conditions he must meet, over the course of the next year, in order to have his conviction lifted. One of the conditions the Court imposed was that he would have no contact or communication whatsoever, either directly or indirectly, with me and my son. Disobeying these terms would not simply result in civil contempt. The consequences were much greater now – if he failed to obey *this* judgment, he could be sent to jail.

Bryan met the conditions of his probation, and his criminal conviction was removed from the forefront of his permanent record the following year; however, it remains, and will always remain, in the background of his permanent record ... for the rest of his life.

As for me? I've gone on with my life in a very positive frame of mind. I no longer look over my shoulder with trepid anticipation as I once did. I'm no longer confined to the role of "The Victim" because I am a survivor. Not only have I learned to trust my own gut instincts once again, but I've learned they were with me all along – I just wasn't listening to them before. I listen to them now, and they always serve me well.

A Letter to My Son

Calvin,

I've been wanting to write you a letter for a very long time, but I've been uncertain about how much information I should provide. That's when I recalled being your age myself, wondering about things that were going on around me at home. One minute, my dad looked fine; the next, he was in the hospital. Adults with good intentions felt that they should protect my feelings by keeping the complete truth from me. So there I was. I saw my family go from "a" to "b" without really knowing how we got there until much later on. It was a very confusing time in my childhood.

Maybe I'm just another adult with good intentions. But having been on both sides of this coin, being the child craving the information and now the adult having to decide how much of it to give, I've come to a conclusion: I believe that the only way a person can deal with something — whether they're eleven or seventy-five — is to know what it is they're dealing with. Period. That's why I'm writing you this letter now. Read what you want. Take from it what you need to take today. And, when you decide you're ready, know that it's here for you in its entirety.

The first thing that I want to make very clear to you is that you were not a "mistake." You were, are, and always will be a gift: the person who helped me see past myself, who made me try a little harder, who showed me the most special kind of love I've ever known.

I don't believe in mistakes, anyway; I believe in choices and decisions. For example, when I chose to move us to Calgary to improve our finances, it worked out as planned. So, did that make it the right thing to do? Or, when I chose to marry and it didn't work out as planned, did that make it a mistake? Or, are decisions just decisions? Choices just choices? And then you deal with whatever happens? Think about that. You can't predict the future.

As you grow older, you're going to start making some choices of your own. Some of them, unfortunately, aren't going to turn out how you expect. Join the club. I happen to be president. And, as president, I want you to know that there isn't a decision you'll make that I won't be there to support and love you through, even if I don't agree with it. You're my son. You can always count on me. I also don't want you to fear making decisions in case they turn out to be a mistake. You'll never know unless you try. As long as your heart is in the right place, your intentions genuine, there are no wrong decisions — only lessons to be learned.

Of course, your decisions need to be informed. It's a maze out there, Calvin. It's easy to get caught up in the excitement when everything is new. You're going to want to experiment and experience everything that's placed in front of you. That's only human. We've all been there, and I do encourage you to try new things, to enjoy your life; however, here are some of the lessons I've learned through the years that will hopefully give you some direction along the way ...

First and foremost, let's talk about teenage sex. Let's talk about losing your self-esteem after giving yourself to someone who doesn't really love you. Let's talk about abandonment, sexually transmitted diseases, abortion, adoption, and parenting under poverty conditions. In the end, it's your body. It's your life. It's your choice. Whatever you do, just make sure you're educated ahead of time. Responsibility goes hand in hand with free will.

I would never change the fact that I had you, Calvin. Watching you grow and learn from that very first ultrasound has been the most wondrous experience of my life. It continues to be (smiling). My only wish is that

I'd been a little older, more financially secure, and in a stable relationship. When the money was tight, I know you saw the brunt of my frustration and impatience as there was no husband to help buffer that stress. When the relationships ended, you had to endure those losses with me. Sometimes I know you didn't want to say good-bye because the man I'd been dating had grown close to your heart, too. Still, you had to let go, and without any say in the matter, whatsoever. That's tough on a little kid, and it's one of the unfortunate realities of single parenting.

I'd like to be able to tell you that you'll never see another man come and go from our lives, but I can't. I can't predict the future. Each time a relationship ends, there's a part of me that says, "That's it — no more," when I think about what it must do to you. Yet, deep down inside, I know I'd be giving you the wrong message if I gave up on dating altogether. If you close your heart completely in this life and keep it protected from all risk, the only thing it will ever know is loneliness. But if you allow yourself to be open to the possibilities of love, you'll know joy and sorrow, passion and pain — and you'll be a better person for it. You'll be alive.

Love will be stressful sometimes, yes. So will many other areas of your life as you mature. There are a lot of different tools in this world that adults use to deal with stress, not all of them good. In a few years — hopefully later rather than sooner! — you're going to be introduced to some of them, probably by some kid at your school. Cigarettes. Alcohol. Drugs. What starts out as seemingly harmless fun often turns into a safety net as you age, a means to medicate yourself from stress. Over time, if you're not careful, these tools only make your problems worse. You can very easily become addicted. Believe me, I know.

So, what is addiction exactly? Well, a friend of mine once likened it to being really thirsty and the only way to quench that thirst is to drink a glass of water. But this is no ordinary water. It leaves you even thirstier, wanting more. And don't kid yourself, Calvin. Some people will try to tell you that there are "soft" drugs and "hard" drugs, and that the softer ones won't really harm you. I disagree. Even with seemingly innocent substances such as cigarettes, alcohol, or marijuana, continued abuse will not only be detrimental to your health in the long run, but to your finances, relationships, and self-esteem. It affects everything over time. When all is known, it's really not worth it.

Don't get me wrong; I'm no prude. I'm not going to sit here and tell you that I'll never touch another drink again in my life. The key is moderation, as one can only learn through personal experience. The key is recognizing that thirst inside yourself and knowing when to stop. Everyone is different. I, for example, can handle alcohol; it doesn't seem to have a grip on me. But cigarettes? Those are my demon. One puff and I'm hooked on them again. I know, through experience, that I can never touch another cigarette now that I've finally quit. I also know you'll have similar experiences of your own — as much as that makes me cringe.

All things considered, I'd like to offer you a natural alternative to dealing with stress: how about crying? Some people are so ashamed to cry — men in particular, I've learned — because they see it as a sign of weakness. "*Real* men don't shed tears." That's simply not true. God gave both men and women the ability to cry for a reason. It allows them to heal. Every one of the tears that falls from our eyes releases more tension from our bodies. That's why some nights, after work, you saw me come home and run a bath immediately. Do you want to know what I was doing in there for an hour? I was crying. And I can't begin to tell you how rejuvenating it was. When I was done, it was as though whatever problem I had was solvable again. There's a lot to be said for tears.

There's also a lot to be said for writing things down. You wouldn't believe the perspective you gain, the negativity you purge from your system when you do this. It is very healing. You don't have to share it with anyone else to reap the benefits; you can choose to throw it away when you're done. For me, there is a strong desire to share my emotions and my experiences with others, because what would have happened if no one else had been willing to share theirs with me? How would I have ever stopped feeling isolated? And, had I continued feeling isolated, how would I ever have healed? I want to give some of that back now.

I just want for you what every parent wants for their child: health and happiness. And I want you to love yourself, Calvin. Don't give into the pressures other people place on you such as how you should look and which activities you should enjoy. Be who you are and be proud of that person, because you'll never truly be happy trying to please everyone else.

You'll also never find self-confidence if you're looking to gain it through other people. It won't come from your teachers, your peers, your future employers, or even from me. It has to come from within you. The way you find self-confidence is by putting yourself out there, taking those risks, and gaining more wisdom through each experience. Some of life's lessons don't feel very positive at the time, so you have to dig a little deeper to gain the right perspective. Like the stories in this letter — they may seem dismal at first glance. But they were all a big part of my own journey to true self-confidence. You see, every time something happened in my life and I survived it, my skin got a little thicker and my spirit grew a little stronger. Because, with each situation, I learned that I *can* survive and I *am* strong. I'm at a point where I can honestly say I love myself, Calvin, and it's not despite all the things that have happened along the way — it's because of them. Remember that the next time you hit a rough spot. Hold on for one more day, and you'll see what I mean.

When I was younger, particularly in my teenage years and early twenties, I didn't always love myself. There were many times when I felt I didn't quite measure up. I was so insecure in who I was, in what I'd done — or not done — with my life. Recognizing that, your uncle Michael brought me a book to read one night called *The Autobiography of St. Thérèse of Lisieux — The Story of a Soul*. There is one passage in that book, in particular, that I like to read when I'm questioning my place in this world. Maybe you'll find some benefit from reading it, too, so I thought I would include it here:

> "... I had wondered for a long time why God had preferences and why all souls did not receive an equal amount of grace. I was astonished to see how He showered extraordinary favours on saints who had sinned against him, saints such as St. Paul and St. Augustine. He forced them, as it were, to accept his graces ... Jesus saw fit to enlighten me about this mystery. He set the book of nature before me and I saw that all flowers he has created are lovely. The splendour of the rose and the whiteness of the lily do not rob the violet of its scent nor the daisy of its simple charm. I realised that if every tiny flower wanted to be a rose, spring would lose its loveliness and there would be no wild flowers to make the meadows gay ... "

Do you see? We can't all be "roses." That's not what God intended. He created athletes, artists, scientists, and philosophers. Some have brown eyes; others have blue. There are men and there are women: some of them right-handed; others, left-handed. The list goes on. We're all different and that's what makes our world the interesting, diverse place that it is. So, be proud of who you are and respect others for who they are, because we all contribute in our own special way. We all have our place in making that meadow beautiful.

And don't just accept yourself. Take good care of yourself. That is so important. Twice in my life, this lesson has been reinforced: first, through watching my mother's marriage; and again, through my own marriage several years later.

If my mom hadn't had her own career, her own means to support herself and her children, then where would she have been when my dad went into the hospital? Sure, some would say, "You can just sell the house and you'll be fine," or "Don't worry, you can always collect insurance." Alas, this was not the case with my mother. Because my father's wound was self-inflicted, there was no disability insurance for her to collect; because "Abby" didn't die right away, there was no life insurance at first, either. And houses don't always sell quickly — it took more than eight months for ours to sell. Things were tough for mom. Suddenly, she found herself trying to cover expenses that were almost double her monthly income. Thank God she'd established her own credit rating through the years. The bank approved a consolidation loan to help manage her debt. Without that, she would have gone bankrupt very quickly. Who knows how much more difficult things would have become.

What about my own marriage? How would I have been able to leave a bad situation without my own source of income? And if hadn't been able to leave, what would have happened to me next? What would have happened to you?

I don't want you to fear marriage; it can be a wonderful thing. Someday, if you decide to marry and have children, and it's important to you or your future wife to stay home with them, I respect that completely. I'm just saying you never know what life is going to throw at you, so keep all your bases covered. Run a day-care or start an Internet business to generate income while you're home with your kids. Just make sure you can take care of yourself and your family either way.

And be safe, Calvin. Beware of whirlwinds. Know that they come in all different ages, sizes, and genders. As a male, you are not any more immune to this kind of hurt than I am. A sure sign of a whirlwind is excessive, irrational jealousy. If you run into this, my best advice to you is to walk away, because when someone behaves this way, they are not expressing their unconditional love for you; rather, they are expressing their intense desire to control you and their inability to control themselves.

When I found myself inside the eye of such a storm not too long ago, I was very torn up inside, not just because there were two children involved but because of my religion. Marriage is supposed to be "for better or for worse, until death do us part." So how could I walk away? What would my family think of me? Well, let me tell you a little something I've learned. I'm not much of a church-goer like my parents or grandparents were, but I do believe in God. And I believe that if your religion makes you choose between your God and your safety, then it's time to seriously rethink your religion. The God I know and love would never put you in that position. He would want you and your children to be happy, healthy, and safe.

I suppose my values differ somewhat from those of my parents. Yours are bound to differ from mine, too. That's natural. The one common thread between all generations is that, at one time or another, we're all torn between our values, not knowing which one holds more clout in our hearts. Whenever you come to that crossroad, uncertain of which path to follow, ask yourself this question: What advice would I give my child? That should give you the answer true to your own core values. Because, in the end, it is the answer that is most important for you — not what other people think.

Love,
Mom

CLASSIC SIGNS OF AN ABUSER / POTENTIAL BATTERER:

Those who batter fit no particular stereotype regarding how they should look or act in public; however, there are certain tendencies to watch for, and they are listed below. A common conception of an abuser is one who is a burly, loud-mouthed, intimidating, unprofessional man. The fact is, they can be blue-collar workers or professionals (such as lawyers, doctors, and police officers). Abusers can be male or female.

- Low self-esteem, which is often displayed outwardly as arrogance (a defense mechanism used to conceal dislike of him/herself)

- Can be very charismatic/personable at times and, to people on the outside, may seem like a great person

- May come on like a whirlwind, claiming love at first sight, flattering you with phrases such as, "I've never loved anyone like this before."

- May push your relationship ahead very quickly, and may try moving you away from familiar friends and surroundings

- Extremely possessive and irrational. He/she may be jealous of who you look at/talk to, of time you spend alone with friends, family, and children

- Will tell you jealousy is a sign of love, or will deny the jealousy altogether

- Tries to control you through isolation (distancing you from family or friends, from going to work or school)

- Calls frequently, or shows up unexpectedly at work or at home (stalking)

- Hypersensitive, easily insulted, and highly argumentative when faced with the slightest criticism/differing opinion

- Dual personality, alternating between extreme tenderness and extreme aggressiveness (a "Jekyll and Hyde" personality.) May fly into a rage without provocation

- Inability to cope with anger and stress, hence the extreme mood swings

- Suspicious, makes accusations, and may often imagine that you are having an affair

- Forcefully controlling

- Refuses to take "no" for an answer

- Believes in using violence to solve problems or have fun, and may have an obsession with weapons

- Abuses alcohol and/or drugs, and will use this as an excuse for his/her abusive behaviour

- May have had other problems with the law that you may or may not be aware of

- Will justify abusive behaviour by projecting blame onto others (such as "You made me do/say it")

- Rants and raves about the injustices in his/her life (again projecting blame onto others)

- Belittles and verbally assaults you with insults, putdowns, threats, et cetera, sometimes disguised as "jokes"

- Will tell you "You take things too literally!" or "Can't you take a joke?" to cover up the shames and threats

- May — or *may not* — come from a family where violence/abusive behaviour was common, and may have learned this behaviour as a child

- Has an intense fear of abandonment

- Has an inability to respect partner's interpersonal boundaries, and a compulsion to violate those boundaries

- May be more violent when partner is pregnant or soon after giving birth

- Denies the abuse or its severity, or seems not to remember, particularly in front of others

- May choose specific items of personal worth to destroy, throw things, or strike walls or furniture as punishment or retaliation

- Will do whatever it takes to force you out (tension building/assault phases) then whatever it takes to bring you back (honeymoon phase), such as apologizing profusely, sending flowers, crying, promising whatever it is he/she knows you want to hear, such as "I'll quit drinking," "I'll go to counselling with you," or "I'll never hurt you again," but does not live up to those promises

- Once you go back to him/her, the cycle repeats: whatever it takes to force you out followed by whatever it takes to bring you back. Over time, the abuse will escalate in intensity

SEVEN TYPES OF ABUSE:

- VERBAL ABUSE: name-calling (constant sarcasm, ridicule, insults, hurtful criticism); threats (to damage or take your property; to harm/kill self, you, children, or family pets; to embarrass you, or hurt your friendships with others)

- EMOTIONAL ABUSE: infidelity; coercion/pressure tactics (rushing you into decisions, making you feel guilty); intimidation (creating fear with facial expressions, tone of voice, gestures, or blocking your movement); isolation (denying privacy, resisting your visitation with friends and family, restricting what you can wear, with whom you can talk, where you can go/can't go, such as work or school); domination (maintaining the power or control in your relationship, always having to be the boss); using the children (sending messages through them, turning them against you by putting you down in front of them, using visitation to continue harassing you)
  * Abuse will often escalate the more you assert yourself.

- PSYCHOLOGICAL ABUSE: stalking, also known as criminal harassment (*any* repeated, unwanted contact, either direct or indirect, that causes you to fear for your safety, or the safety or someone known to you. Some examples include obsessive letter writing, emailing, or telephone calls/hang-ups, following or surveillance, showing up uninvited to your home or workplace, sending unwanted gifts such as flowers or candy, besetting or watching the places you frequent)
  * This behaviour does not have to be explicitly threatening to be potentially dangerous.
  ** Stalking in the workplace can be interpreted

as a form of sexual harassment by Human Rights. Criminal harassment/sexual harassment is illegal, and employers can be held accountable along with the perpetrator if this behaviour occurs on their property.

- FINANCIAL ABUSE: controlling family finances (concealing joint assets or money, spending all the family money, keeping you impoverished by not allowing you to earn a living)

- PHYSICAL ABUSE: pushing, slapping, hitting, kicking, choking, pulling your hair, biting, using weapons, tying you up, locking you in a room, preventing you from sleeping, harming your pets, breaking into your vehicle/house or destroying your property
  * If someone *physically* damages any of your personal property, or *physically* throws something at you, even if it doesn't directly hit you, this is a form of *physically* abusing you.

- SEXUAL ABUSE: also known as sexual harassment (sexist statements/behaviours that insult or degrade you, displaying sexually exploitive or pornographic materials that offend you, unwanted sexual advances or invitations, demands that you perform sexual acts you are not comfortable with, subtle or overt promises of rewards — or threats of punishment — if sexual advances are not reciprocated, stalking you, or sexually assaulting you such as touching you inappropriately, kissing you against your wishes, or raping you)
  * The statements/behaviours mentioned above do not have to be explicitly sexual in nature to constitute sexual harassment. Insistent, unwanted contact, requests for dinner/drinks, or other invitations can be considered sexual harassment — as can sending unwanted gifts.

** Mutual flirtation is not considered sexual harassment. As not everyone will be offended by the same statements/behaviours, or by displays of various materials (such as posters of scantily clad women/men), it is important for you to let the other person know that you are offended by asking him/her to stop. It is also, therefore, important that the accused respect these wishes to discontinue the statements/behaviours, or remove the materials, to prevent a complaint being made against them.
*** While all forms of sexual harassment are illegal, sexual assault and stalking are two forms that fall under the criminal code of the legal system. If convicted, the accused may face jail time and will have a criminal record that will follow him/her for life.

- SYSTEM ABUSE: violating restraining orders and/or child custody agreements, lying to the police, therapists, or the courts about you

ISBN 141201860-9